THE OFFICIAL NOVELIZATION BY
DAMIEN CASEY

BASED ON THE SCREENPLAY BY
J.R. BOOKWALTER

Encyclopocalypse Publications
www.encyclopocalypse.com

VITALLY IMPORTANT INTRODUCTION

BY MIKE WATT

Rumor and Innuendo to be officially blamed on James L. Edwards™

J.R. Bookwalter's feature film debut, *The Dead Next Door*, was an audacious ode to Romero, aided by *The Evil Dead* gang of Raimi and Campbell, and managed to pull off some pure miracles of Super-8mm filmmaking. It opened a lot of doors for all of us, but especially J.R. himself. The tall, gawky never-say-die-out-loud, eager young go-getter, standing 6'2, (sometimes as much as 6'4 depending on how level the ground), soon found himself embroiled on another cinematic adventure.

Which brings us to *Robot Ninja*.

While *The Dead Next Door* was rightfully heralded in the gore mags, *Robot Ninja*, produced by the King of the Scream Queens, David DeCoteau, is a genuine oddity that was largely overlooked in its time. While earlobe deep into post on *Dead Next Door*, J.R. was approached by Dave D. to write and direct a $15K horror movie. $15K was a lot of money back (now) then, but not a large amount to make a movie. Not when you're trying to recreate a reality wherein a deranged comic book artist dons the lethal garb of his own creation to take on a crazed mob of teenaged psychopaths. The indie spirit is indominable, however. Do your best with what you've got.

If you yourself have never been under the gun at 3am with an exhausted punch-drunk cast and crew trying to get that last *goddamned* gore gag to work, your criticism will fall on deaf ears. *Robot Ninja* is the movie that tells every other indie filmmaker that everything will be all right.

It was a rarity on VHS (apparently… I had three copies at one point) and is quite the collectible now. While I'm taking a snarky tone here, *Robot Ninja* is not a *bad movie*. It's not a "so bad it's good," a backhanded compliment I never liked. It's unique. What's more, beneath the "low budget" complaints everyone has, *Robot Ninja* has a lot of pure Bookwalter. His off-beat humor, his love of comics and his dexterity with ultra-violence (whoever "Lance Randas" is, he knows not to linger on an effect and keeps the pace brisk).

What usually stands out for me with a Bookwalter movie is the story. Even those ultra-cheapies he bandied together under the *Bad Movie Police* banner (listen to the commentaries on some of these and tell me you don't wanna give self-deprecating J.R. a big hug), Bookwalter approached with a unique sensibility. Sometimes it was "how fast can I shoot this and do I have enough cardboard left to build the sets?" His stories are always whacked-out lumps of Bookwalter id. Anything goes, and there's always an internal logic.

Perhaps the film version of *Robot Ninja* was inevitable, but an infinite number of monkeys couldn't have churned out the final version in the exact same way, and Damien here deserves applause for presenting something purely visual for the prose world. Seriously. *Put the book down and clap, goddamn it!*

Have a good time with this one. It captures the movie to the letter, which means there's a tiny chunk of J.R.'s soul within this book as well. Perhaps screaming to be let free, but within nonetheless.

Mike Watt, 2024
Screenwriter of *Weregrrl, Severe Injuries, Demon Divas and the Lanes of Damnation*

ROBOT NINJA

1

"Five hundred dollars and some middle-aged soccer mom? That's all you bozos got me?" Esmeralda Evil is upset, downright pissed off. She sent her three goons to rob the local sporting goods store and they came back with pocket change and the owner's wife.

"Yeah, but," says Dastardly Dan, "maybe we can hold her hostage?"

"Plus," says Horrid Harry, "we've got all this drug money!"

"Oh yeah!" says Esmeralda as she throws her head back and lets out a cackle that rivals the Wicked Witch of the West.

The villains laugh and slap each other's backs.

Outside, something stalks through the freshly cut lawn.

A force of Justice, a force for good.

With one foot placed in front of the other, justice strides to the front door and kicks it in.

"Curses!" shouts Esmeralda. "Get 'im boys!"

One of the henchmen, Dan, leaps forward toward the intruder and is met with the flat of a combat boot in the chest. Five of his ribs shatter on impact; one pierces his heart instantly killing him. The blood fills his body and coats his insides like a water balloon ready to burst.

Another wields a knife but is shoved out of the way by an

enraged Esmeralda; this was her brother the intruder just eliminated. She rushes forward with a knife of her own, but the intruder has a surprise. The intruder slashes his arm fast, the three blades extending from his glove slice through the flesh of Esmeralda's chest. She falls in a heap of blood and shredded flesh.

Harry leaps forward to protect Esmerelda and catches the claws across his face. His severed nose slides across the floor in the path of Dan. Dan's foot comes down on the severed sniffer like a banana peel in a *Three Stooges* routine. As Dan falls forward toward the masked avenger, he feels the tip of a boot kick his chest and send him flying backward. His head strikes a metal pole splitting his skull and killing him instantly.

On the floor, Mary Mercy struggles against the tape her captors used to hold her arms and legs together. The masked man swipes his claws out and frees her from her bindings. She stands and takes in his appearance; dressed in all black with a mask made of metal creating a sort of wrap around his eyes and mouth. She can't decide if he's here to help or cause more problems.

"Who are you?" she asks.

The man who caught the boot tries to attack the masked man from behind. The guy in the mask shoots his fist back. The metal holding the claw to his hand shatters the man's nose sending fragments of bone into his brain.

"I am the Robot Ninja," the masked man says pointing his finger at Mary. "And remember kids, drugs are not cool."

Mary leaps up and wraps her arms around the robot ninja, "Robot Ninja! You're my hero!"

"No," says Robot Ninja. "Courageous citizens like you are the real heroes."

The scene freezes and laughter can be heard.

Two people sit on a couch watching this scene play out on TV in front of them.

"Boy," says the man. "Best idea I ever had letting NBC have the rights to this."

"And to think," says a woman. "Lenny Miller was SO opposed to the show being all CGI like the Marvel movies!"

"Lenny Miller is just a pretentious artist. He can't STAND the fact that everyone is saying Robot Ninja is the new Iron Man!"

"He doesn't get how much money we can make; the social media engagement has been through the roof!"

"I tried to tell him, I said, 'Look, Lenny. *The Walking Dead*, *The Avengers*, Robert BATTINSON: what do they all have in common? Money baby! Money!' He didn't get it. He said something about 'my artistic vision' blah blah blah and 'the fans expect' blah blah blah. The fans hated *Black Adam* too! But guess what? They all went and watched it! It made money! Who cares about artistic whatchamacrap!"

The man pushes 'Play' on the remote. On screen, Mary rubs the side of Robot Ninja's face and says, "I wish I could see what was behind that mask..."

"Fans were outraged!" says the woman. "We've gotten a million tweets and comments about how Robot Ninja would NEVER be a part of a cheap romantic angle... They'll still tune in next week though!"

"It's Batfleck all over again!" says the man. "Batman doesn't kill people in the comics, but he did in the movie and sequels you schmucks paid your hard-earned money to see!"

"I wonder what Lenny thinks of this week's episode..."

"Lenny will get over it! Hey, you look like the kind of woman who could do some interesting tricks with a tube of lipstick."

Lenny Miller is absolutely pissed about this week's episode. The kind of pissed that is usually accompanied by some form of legal settlement and a pack of lawyers. He's spent years upon years of his life investing all of his time into the *Robot Ninja* franchise. Now this, this bullshit show. His life's work has been shat all over.

Last night he got a text from his mom that said, *"LENNY! The show is everything we knew it would be!!!! Your father said it reminds him of Captain America! XOXOXO"*

If he wasn't pissed off before that, he was then. Who wants their Baptist parents to love their TV show? Boring assholes, that's who! He stood up and moved toward the TV with a purpose. He was going to leave a size eleven Nike footprint right in the middle of it. As he was about to kick out with all of his might he remembered Netflix was dropping the entire fourth season of *Odd Happenings* in a week and he needed a TV to binge.

He settled for giving the television set the sternest middle finger he possibly could.

That was last night.

Currently, he's sitting outside of the TV station's headquarters planning to go inside and make some heads cave in over the shit he watched last night. Bad writing from someone who had to be a toddler who also never met a human; a shitty sub plot that tried to make the viewer feel sympathy for the villain; and, worst of all, a stupid romance angle.

He couldn't tell if the *Robot Ninja* series was actually live-action or some weird animation. That's how much CGI was used. To make matters worse, some of it was bad CGI. It looked like the graphics from a PlayStation game. Not the PS5 either, the original PlayStation. The blocky one. Was there some sort of Lego tie in? That's the only thing that makes sense. Why else would it be as blocky as it is?

Goddamnit he hated it.

He grips his steering wheel as he takes the turns way too fast. He can feel the plastic rubbing off into his palms from the friction. He runs through the last red light and flashes a security guard his badge, then his middle finger. He starts to feel a little bad about that; the guard didn't do anything.

He slams his car door and makes his way across the parking lot. He steps in front of a car that slams on its brakes and lays on the horn. He slams his hands on the hood like he could stop the vehicle with his strength.

"Pedestrians have right of way, asshole!" Lenny says while giving this car a middle finger of less sternness than the security guard. He feels bad about that instantly; this guy deserved way worse! He would have to remember to buy the guard lunch... or at least call and apologize... maybe just send an email.

He barges through the front door and walks up to the desk. Each step he takes radiating of pissed-off; the impact almost breaks the laws of physics and has a smell. He's a walking time bomb ready to explode.

"Um, hi, yes, I'm here to see my agent... Rip," he says as politely as possible to the young guy sitting behind the desk. He doesn't want to fuck up and flip this guy off and have another situation like the guard.

Still fuming, yet always falling victim to the millennial curse of being polite to a stranger.

"Who are you exactly?" the guy asks.

"I'm Lenny Miller."

"…and that means what to me?"

"Listen here, booger dick. I created *Robot Ninja*, then your company went and fucked it up. And why are you being so rude? We millennials and Gen Z'ers have a code. We have to be polite to strangers, goddamn you!"

The guy looks at Lenny then picks up his phone and dials a number. He hangs up the phone and says, "yeah, Rip said he'll talk to you."

Lenny storms off through the doors in the back of the waiting area.

"Wrong door!" yells the receptionist.

Lenny comes back past the desk and presents another very stern middle finger before making his way through another door and down a hallway; he's already convinced himself he has no reason to feel bad about that one. He passes an open doorway with two security guards inside. They're watching *Robot Ninja* and having a lengthy conversation about how this character ties into the other characters the company has made shows based on.

Lenny shudders in fan theory and moves on. As he moves down the hallway, he can almost feel their shitty blog posts passing through his body like an electric current while they upload to the internet. *Mother fuckers think everything is connected,* Lenny thinks.

He slings open another door and sees Rip and three other dickheads standing around a desk laughing the kind of laugh that only people who just robbed someone can laugh.

"Lenny! How you doing?" Rip says.

"Cut the shit, Rip. What's the deal with the show?" Lenny says.

"Great stuff right! This is the shows director, Joey McHighster, and this is the producer, Greg Lange."

"Yeah, yeah, kid," says the man named Joey. "Hand me that wipe. The wipe. No, the wipe!"

He's standing behind a man wearing a set of headphones, as he asks for a wipe a third time, he smashes the man's head into the desk. "So, Rip says you got some sort of a problem with the show. Cut the shit and tell me about it."

"Lenny, tell him!" says Rip.

"C'mon, Rip. You're the agent. I'm the comic book artist," Lenny says.

"Now look, McHighster. We think-"

"No, YOU look," McHighster interrupts by pointing his cigar in Rip's face. "Amsteel Comics contracted us to make this show. Right, Greg?"

"Yeah, whatever," says Greg.

"Right. We saw a lot of potential in the character. Lenny is the most popular artist since that loser invented that *Mutant Teenage Turtle Ninja* crap. This could be our company's path to starting a cinematic universe. Cinematic universes are all people care about anymore, right Greg?"

"Yeah, whatever," says Greg.

"We plant a few little Easter eggs here and there. The fans go fuckin' wild over the Easter eggs. Then we slowly show how Robot Ninja and the other stand-alone heroes we bought are actually a part of the same universe. Marvel has that Avengers crap everyone loves, right, Greg?"

"Yeah, whatever 3000," says Greg.

"You gave us certain… creative freedoms with the character. We're taking advantage of that to make a new cinematic universe. Think of the marketing! Think of the posts! When we show Robot Ninja in one of these other assholes shows, think of the amount of clicks and posts we'll get! All we have to do is pull that one scene where someone says, 'I know who we can ask for help' and the other guy says, 'You don't mean…' and then, BLAMMO! ROBOT MOTHER FUCKING NINJA IS TRENDING. The engagement will be unreal!"

"You know," Lenny says, "you people don't give a shit about *Robot Ninja*. Do whatever you want with the TV show. It's all bullshit anyway. I'll do what I want with the comics. Cut out his guts and make them look like glittery ribbons for all I care."

As Lenny gives another of his trademark stern middle fingers, he hears McHighster say, "The comic people want you to follow our lead now, Lenny! We're the ones making them money!"

As his voice fades, Lenny pauses by the open door with the security guards to collect his thoughts. He thinks about how fucked up this all is. He had to scratch and claw to even get the comic off the ground in the first place. No one wanted a comic with realistic violence and portrayals of real crimes. All anyone wanted back then was a guy pretending to be a flying rodent fighting a guy who thinks he's the funniest man in the room. Lenny loved that shit but thought he could make something more real; make a hero the world really needed.

"Hey," says one of the guards, "give us the inside scoop. We saw a quarter from 1986 in this episode. Everyone knows that Cat Karen has a quarter from that year she wears as a necklace. Does this mean Cat Karen and Robot Ninja are in the same universe?"

Lenny can feel his face turning red. He feels like someone turned the heat on in his brain.

"What about this one?" says the other guard. "Robot Ninja went to a deli and the guy in front of him ordered a vegetarian sub. Now hear me out. Rabbits don't eat meat, right? And we've never once seen Rabbit Warrior eat on his show. Could that have been Rabbit Warrior?"

Lenny snaps.

He lets out the loudest shriek he could find in his body and grabs the TV set with both hands. He throws it like a frisbee against the back wall.

"I'LL SHOW ALL OF YOU WHAT *ROBOT NINJA* IS ABOUT!" Lenny yells before storming off.

The two men give the empty doorway their version of Lenny's stern middle finger.

"What now?"

"I dunno. Want to spend more time looking up fan theories instead of actually reading the source material for ourselves?"

3

———

Tonight was the night.

Susan knew it.

Harvey didn't order the country fried steak at Rachel's unless he had something big planned. She had waited, and waited, and waited some more for Harvey to ask her to marry him. She had been banking on it ever since she found out he was going to school to become a pastor.

She didn't even realize there was a school for that, but she found herself all smiles that there was. If there wasn't a school, then any old con artist could lie and say they were a pastor just to rip off little old ladies.

No way, not Harvey.

Harvey used to help sister Eileen carry her famous grape jelly meatballs into church every Sunday. Sure, she gave him a crisp twenty every time... but Harvey didn't take it until Eileen insisted.

The best part about Harvey FINALLY proposing to her was now she could be the pastor's wife. Harvey had already been told he was taking over the First Baptist Church. The church that Susan knew had a youth group of twenty-five, twenty-two of which had parents who made close to seven digits a year.

A little field trip here where she lies about the costs.

A little dinner there with a bloated grocery bill.

Kids are idiots and their parents are even dumber when they want their kids to stop crying about everything they want.

Susan was going to make damn sure she had all the money she could possibly want, thanks to these greasy, grubby, ugly, shit stained underwear, stretched out shirt collar, rich kids.

Her plan of holding out on sex was working out great, too. It was all Harvey could think about. Even now as he took a bite of his gravy covered fried meat, his eyes were locked on to her tits like they were the face of some monster that would eat you up if you broke eye contact. Not too far off base truthfully, if he broke eye contact and started thinking for himself, he may see that Susan was using him.

She couldn't stand the thought of his weird looking dick inside her. She pulled it out of his pants one night, just looking to tease him a little bit, but when she saw it, she gasped. The thing was at least ten inches long and had a weird curve to it. It always looked like it was trying to look up at the ceiling.

Susan wanted to ask it if it was looking to buy the place.

How could something like that even fit inside her?

Wouldn't the curvature be a bit... odd?

She wouldn't have to find out for a while, and for that she was thankful to Jesus, God, and the Holy Spirit high above.

Across from her, Harvey had different plans. As he chomped away at the steak, he couldn't take his eyes off Susan. The way her sweater lightly lay against the mounds on her chest. He had seen her wear this sweater at least once a week, but for some reason tonight was different. Susan has been sending mixed signals for about a month. Ever since she saw his... thing... she's been acting different. She had to want it. When she seen it, something primal had to have awoken. Now she had to have more.

That's why tonight, he planned to go all the way. She was excited about something too; she never ordered the lasagna unless it was a special occasion.

The waitress drops off their bill and Susan asks, "Are you ready?"

He looked at her, smiled, and said, "I've been waiting for this night for so long."

As they exit Rachel's, both ecstatic for two different reasons, three pairs of eyes watch.

———

Three predators sit inside a black van stalking their prey. They watch as Harvey holds the car door for Susan and pumps his fist into the air. They're going to fuck these people up in the name of nothing but chaos.

Gody Sanchez nods; her partner, Sculley pulls out.

As Harvey leans in for a kiss, Revelle leans out the sliding door and yanks Susan in by the arm. The van pulls off leaving a stunned Harvey behind.

Harvey watches as the van does a circle around the parking lot with his girlfriend. *They must be bringing her back*, he thinks; *this must be some new viral video trend or something.*

He watches the van circle the lot like a shark circling its prey. He starts to laugh a little as it pulls up beside him with the side door open.

"Hardee har har," he says, "you've had your laughs. Now, if you don't mind-"

Harvey's interrupted as he's pulled into the van and slammed to the ground.

He looks over and sees a man in a denim jacket and red bandana straddling Susan.

"Show that bitch a thing or two, Revelle," says Gody as she climbs on top of him.

"You know it, Gody."

Harvey and Susan struggle against their captors; both are too filled with special occasion dinners to do anything about what's happening.

"Ah, fuck!" yells the voice of the driver.

"What the fucks the matter, Sculley?" asks Gody.

"Goddamn radiator is blown!"

"I told Revelle to fix that! I even gave him money!"

"I told you I ain't no goddamn Mr. Goodwrench," says Revelle. "I gave the money to my cousin Keith, and he said he fixed it up."

"Your cousin Keith... is this the same cousin who took my cousin Lisa out for a night on the town two days ago?"

"Yeah! That's him!"

"That was our money, you fucking idiot!"

"Why would he take Lisa to buy a radiator?"

"Sculley, pull the fuck over!"

Sculley is famous among the gang for fuck ups like this. Gody can't take it. She said she would take both Sculley and Revelle under her wing if they would stop continuously fucking up. That remains to be seen. A promise is a promise, and she'll keep trying as hard as she can to make these two worth a shit.

Gody was raised by a single father who had one single job – killing the shit out of people. He was one of the best hitmen in the world and he made sure to take Gody out on hits as soon as she was old enough to hold a gun. Gody's father was a killer, and her mother was death. She learned all the spots in a human body that caused pain; she knew the spots that caused instant death. She worked her way up through the ranks of a local gang until she was in charge of a bigger chapter. She killed the last person who had the job, then broke the replacement's neck. She didn't even give a fuck about the power, she just wanted to hurt others. She was misery incarnate with a doctorate in fucking people up.

In short, Gody Sanchez was one bad mother fucker.

Revelle and Sculley, on the other hand, were bad mother fuckers in a different sense; a derogatory sense. They sucked ass at everything they did, so the gang leader, in his infinite nameless wisdom, stuck them with his top assassin. The boys were quickly regretting leaving behind their parents' fancy homes in Los Angeles and glamorizing a life of crime. They watched *Snatch* one time and decided they were deviants. They had no idea that people like Gody existed. People who lived to hurt; people who were born to be reapers. Gody looked at violence the same way a kid looks at a slide: nothing but joy and excitement.

She was their mentor, and she scared the shit out of them. When Gody told them to do something, they kept the receipts and did extra credit.

She was with them this time, so they knew they had to try extra hard. They would reassure each other with eye contact every step of the way and hope no one showed up to ruin the night.

4

Lenny Miller is still pissed off. The kind of pissed that couldn't be calmed; not with a Happy Meal, a massage, or even money. He spent most of his life agreeing with everyone to avoid conflict, so now when he finally snapped, he snapped BIG. His life was spent avoiding making others mad or upset. An empath of the highest order, Lenny spent much of his time saying, "That's cool with me! Whatever you want." It wasn't that he didn't like confrontation; it was more that he cared that deeply about others. He didn't want his dinner choice of pizza to interfere with someone's craving for tacos. He'd take the loss on that one as long as others were smiling.

This is what initially got him into the world of comic books. Most heroes only cared about making the world around them better. They had no selfish motivation. If they had to sacrifice their lives to improve the lives of others, they would. Lenny admired that. After years of being told he was odd for caring about others, how could he not?

These heroes were fully capable of taking what they wanted from anyone. They were the most powerful beings on Earth, yet they used their power to help others, not to take whatever they wanted.

Robot Ninja was the embodiment of that mindset. Was he a little more violent? Fuck yes. But with good reason. Lenny was sick to death of seeing people watch superhero movies every single weekend, and then go out into the world and take advantage of everyone around them. Robot Ninja stood as a shining neon light that said, "Hey, if you're an asshole, you're going to get your dick knocked in the dirt."

Was that the right mindset to have? Probably not.

Which is what made *Robot Ninja* special: the internal conflict between what is right and what is wrong. How far is too far to ensure your vision of a perfect world is maintained?

Lenny thought about these things. He thought about how far he would go to protect the idea of *Robot Ninja*. He thought of some stupid fuck cutting someone else off in traffic with a *Robot Ninja* bumper sticker while he punched the steering wheel, asking himself why he hired an agent named Rip Me'off.

Should have been a goddamn sign, that one.

He still didn't get why those assholes wanted to take his comic, the comic heralded as "fresh" and "completely different from anything else!" by critics, and make it into another boring copy-and-paste version of what Marvel is doing. Didn't DC try that and fall on their faces miserably?

Putting *Robot Ninja* in the *Cat Karen* series was a sure-fire way to piss off the *Robot Ninja* fan base that Lenny had spent close to a decade building trust with. In today's comic world, it's near impossible to do such a thing. The gap between creator and fan has never been bigger. Most creators are looking for their huge *Walking Dead* style payday, and most fans are expecting the creators to do just that and change everything they love about the characters.

The relationship between a comic book fan and the characters they love is a strong one. You don't fuck around and change Aquaman into a guy who has both his parents. You don't change the dynamic he has that makes him stuck between two worlds; the surface, and the ocean. You can change how he looks; you can change how he talks. But these fundamental things—like Batman never killing— if you fuck with those, the fans are pissed.

Changing Wonder Woman's origin from being made of clay, to being the daughter of Zeus changes the whole character and makes poor Dianna less relatable to her fans. These fucks have watched it happen before; they've seen creators fall because of this shit. Here they are though, never learning. You live and you learn, but in the case of TV execs, you live, and you live.

Fans find things in a comic book character they connect with on a deeper level than the art on the page. They hold these character traits close to their hearts and take any change to them deeply personal.

As they should.

Lenny was a fan too.

He would spend hours reading about how Wonder Woman was here by accident, but still trying to save humanity from itself. He read about Swamp Thing trying to find and connect to the humanity he lost time and time again. He held the story of Peter Parker close to his heart. A man who had terrible things happen to him and decided to use his power not for vengeance, but to make sure it didn't happen again. When he started gaining notoriety as an artist he clung to *Shazam* like a Bible; Lenny feeling just as out of place as a popular comic creator as Billy Batson did when he turned into a hero. These characters weren't something you fucked around with. You didn't ruin people's connections to heroes.

Now his hero, his pride and joy, his Robot Ninja was just that; a shell of the hero he was on paper. A watered-down asshole who knew some Jiu Jitsu. Another cheap *Batman* rip-off with bad CGI.

In his peak of anger, he pulls up behind a van stopped on the side of the road. He sighs and remembers how Iron Man uses his notoriety to help and grabs his phone. He heads to social media to send out a post asking if anyone with a knowledge of cars is close to this spot and willing to help a stranger.

As he's about to hit the send button he hears a woman scream from inside the van. He closes the app and dials 911.

"Hello? Yeah, I think there's someone in trouble. I'm on the corner of Moore and Perez."

He sits there for a minute before seeing four people stumble out of the side of the van.

Three men, two women get out of the van.

One man and woman are held by gun-point and knife-point as they're being shoved around by their obvious captors.

Lenny opens his door and walks toward them, his body language saying, *"I do not have time for this shit."*

The man holding the woman hostage at the end of a knife sees Lenny and says, "Don't come any fucking closer man. I'll fucking gut her!"

Lenny walks right through his threats and punches him in the face.

"Run, Susan!" yells the male hostage.

Lenny feels a boulder hit square in his nuts. He doubles over feeling like he's going to puke.

As he's falling, he sees the female captor holding the man pull a gun and shoot a round across the field at the running Susan.

The bullet smashes into the back of Susan's head and explodes out of her mouth. Bits of teeth, tongue, and gum fly into the air. She stands there too shocked to die, and too dead to run. Her hands move up to her mouth and explore the wound. Her fingers going in and out of the spots where teeth used to be like she's performing some sort of self-dentistry. Suddenly, another round hits her in the shoulder, then another in her back. She falls forward in a slump. She goes from young and full of life to pile of inanimate meat in approximately three seconds.

Lenny feels the boots of the two male captors connecting with his face and stomach as he lay on the ground. He feels like a pinball going back and forth between the paddles that are the men's feet. Judging by how badly the one side feels, he's positive one of them is wearing steel toes.

"No! Susan!" yells the male hostage as he breaks free of his captor only to be stabbed in the stomach by the other man. He bends over as his attacker continues to send the knife in and out of his stomach like it's the penis of a sex addict that's been denied even masturbation for a century. He feels his organs leaving his body through the wound, still being stabbed as they exit. This is some sort of a masochist's food factory.

The hostage, Harvey, lays down as his attacker, Revelle, continues stabbing and yelling.

The last thing Lenny sees is the flashing red and blue lights of a cop car reflected on the back of the van.

"What a fucking mess!" he hears someone yell. "This one's alive!"

With that, Lenny blacks out.

5

———

Dr. Goodknight wasn't at all pleased to pick Lenny up from the hospital. He had told him over the phone he shouldn't be proud of the shit he pulled. Lenny wouldn't shut up; he kept saying he could use it all for *Robot Ninja*.

"I'll show those ad exec, social media click, boner headed fucks what *Robot Ninja* is all about," Lenny said on the car ride back to his place.

"I'm sure you will, Leonard, I'm sure you will," said Dr. Goodknight.

Lenny thought, for a guy who wears a bright ass yellow hat that states, "I thought I was wrong once, but I was mistaken," he sure says my name wrong every goddamned time.

Maybe he was just old-school like that?

Lenny spent a good chunk of the car ride home trying to figure out what the Doc's deal was.

He came into Lenny's life when he was in high school. Lenny took his science and robotics elective his Junior year. Ever since then, the Doc became a sort of uncle figure for Lenny. Now that his parents had moved two states over, he spent more and more time with Dr. Goodknight; Lenny needed that parental guidance.

Goodknight said he could see something special in Lenny, something good.

Lenny thinks he's full of shit.

They pull up to the curb of Lenny's apartment and he steps out. He makes his way up the stairs and to his door. When he opens it, he waves to Goodknight who will sit there waiting all day for Lenny to get into the apartment.

What makes a guy who isn't even blood care so much?

He shakes his head in his bedroom; he hasn't stopped thinking about the strange name thing even when Doc dropped him off.

I just wish he'd stop calling me Leonard, he thinks as he draws.

He recreates the scene from last night panel-by-panel; he heard the voices screaming out for help. He could hear the gun shooting Susan over and over and over again.

His balls began to ache at the memory of the physical and emotional pain he felt in these moments the previous night.

He realizes he would do anything to get these fuckers. To him they had become a stand-in for the network execs, for his agent, for everyone who tried to make him eat a helping of watered-down *Robot Ninja*. These people had become every single asshole in the world who only cared about their needs and desires. Fuck everyone else. These people were the lowest of the low. The most selfish of the most selfish. Human waste.

He tries to shake the thought from his head. It isn't productive for him to think about people like that. The pain in the side of his face reminds him that that is exactly how he should be thinking of people like that.

"I'll show these fucks what *Robot Ninja* is all about," he says to himself. "I'll show each and every one of them you don't fuck around with Robot Ninja or Lenny Miller."

Meanwhile, across town in a dark basement, Gody has Revelle and Scully tied to two chairs. Their arms are outstretched onto a table where they're tied together.

"My father used to do this to me when I fucked up," Gody

says. She pulls a hammer from the back pocket of her jeans. She thinks about that goody fucking good Samaritan that tried to stop her fun. She thinks of all the doctors, teachers, mental health experts who tried to tell her she shouldn't find joy in the sound of breaking bones.

She lifts the hammer and sends it crashing down onto the stacked fingernails of Revelle and Scully. She feels her spirits lifting as they cry out in pain. She turns the hammer over and pries the remaining nail from both fingers. Their cries are orgasmic to her ears.

Wait until I find this fuck, she thinks. *I won't even have to make up some stupid ass story about my dad; stupid assholes believe it; don't they realize my fingers wouldn't work anymore?*

6

———

Toothpicks taste like shit. Why does anyone chew on these things? It does make me look more serious though. Like I'm a man who means business, a man with whom not to fuck, a man who could have a ladder match for the intercontinental title at WrestleMania. Fuck, ok, now I see why people chew on these things. I look like a total bad ass. That's a fair trade for a little bit of bad wood taste. Maybe I should start chewing on popsicle sticks. The bigger the chunk of wood, the badder the ass, right? Nah, that may honestly be too far. Kind of like a clown shoe.

These are the thoughts passing through Stanley Kane's head as he listens to this Marty Coleslaw dipshit try to explain that his comic, *Bayou Thing,* is totally different, and not at all exactly the same as Lenny Miller's *Bog Thing.*

"Hey," Stanley says, pointing his toothpick at Marty in some insane power move. "These aren't too bad. Not too bad at all."

The pages of art look like a toddler with two broken arms drew them. There are scribbles, scratches, weird highlights, and for some reason, all of the hands look like gelatin.

"You think so?" asks Marty in his voice that sounds like a kid going through puberty who also smokes five packs a day. "It took me hours to get it right!"

"Yeah, not bad at all. Only, here's the thing. We have an artist,

23

Leonard Miller. I'm sure you've heard of him. Actually I'm positive you've read his comic, *Bog Thing*. I say that because these panels, well, I'll be frank,"

"I thought your name was Stanley?"

"Huh?"

"You said you'll be Frank."

Stanley stares at the guy, trying not to slap the taste out of his mouth. What is this? A bad *Three Stooges* routine?

"Yeah, funny," Stanley says. "What I was saying is these panels look really, and I mean REALLY, close to the panels from the last issue of *Bog Thing*. They kind of look like you traced over AI art."

"Oh yeah, that's because I wanted to make my own version. So, I just sort of redrew them in a different style; my style, as you can see."

"I can see. The thing is, Leonard Miller has a copyright on the character—"

Stanley is interrupted by Marty slamming his hand on the desk; the sound is like a canon going off in the quiet office.

"LEONARD MILLER!" yells Marty. "COPYRIGHT LAW THIS, COPYRIGHT LAW THAT! I think copyright law is bullshit! I should be able to take influence from Leonard's work and create a tribute! Do you see my hands? They're insured for ten thousand dollars each!"

"Hey, hey, hey," says Stanley. "I got no problem with tribute or influence. This though, this looks like you asked Leonard if you could copy his homework. You can't just make money off someone else's work, Marty."

"Amsteel is the biggest, well, third biggest comic company in the world! They won't even notice! I'll release it myself!"

"You brought the comic to the third biggest comic book company you're ripping off. I really wouldn't publish that. Think of it this way, your character, Lobster Larry..."

"Hey! You want Larry?"

"No, no fucking way, Marty. What if someone just scanned

your pages, colored them differently, and made money selling them?"

"That's stealing my work, goddamnit!"

"So, you see, this is exactly what you're trying to do to Leonard."

"It's completely different!" He slams his hand down on the desk again and again with each word that follows. "THE THIRD BIGGEST COMIC BOOK COMPANY DESERVES IT!"

As he says it, he lets rip the hardest hit he could possibly find. Unfortunately for his ten thousand dollar insured hand, there's a giant needle standing face up that Stanley uses for receipts. The needle slides through Stanley's palm like it's a receipt for a Big Mac and a large fry.

Stanley jumps up and lets out a howl.

"You'll be seeing this in print! Fuck you! And fuck Leonard Miller! Fuck copyright law!" Marty screams all of this as he gathers his artwork and heads to the door. In his frustration he bashes his head against the door when he opens it too fast. He grunts and slams the door behind him.

Stanley shakes his head.

Just then the door opens slightly again, and Marty's art is fed through; the door is slammed again as Marty pulls his art back through the closed door in an attempt to straighten the wrinkles and folds he created.

Jesus H Christ, this guy is a walking, living, breathing Three Stooges rip off, Stanley thinks.

He rubs his temples; he can't figure out how people are so damn stupid sometimes.

A knock on his door breaks his thoughts of murder, and in walks his assistant, Ms. Barbeau.

Thank God, Stanley thinks, *after that shit show I could use a few seconds of eye therapy.*

"Here's the new issue of *Lizard Boy*, Mr. Kane," says Ms. Barbeau as she walks into the office.

Stanley pauses for a minute and takes in her full appearance.

Crop top, thick framed glasses, platinum blonde hair, all the right parts in all the right sizes. *Yeah,* he thinks, *I'm glad I hired her over that guy who worked at DC for twenty years.*

"Have you seen these?" He asks.

"*Robot Ninja,* huh? Wait! These don't look anything like the TV show. They look way too violent!" She bends forward when she says it. He watches her eyes scan the page for half a second before he realizes there is a better view. He stares at her cleavage and imagines what it would be like to just slide his hand in there. She'd probably like it. She'd probably let him take her right here on this desk.

"Way too violent!" She says it loud enough to make her boss think she's on his side. The truth is she thinks this is better than the show. But, saying that will piss her boss off, and then how would she use her assets and his love of them to get an audition as Cat Karen for season two? Men are easy. Just make them think they have a chance of putting that rancid little thing in you and they'll give you anything you want. This one was even easier; all it took was low-cut shirts to get this promotion.

"Exactly. Can you get Leonard Miller on the phone for me?"

"You got it, chief!"

"One more thing. Has anyone ever told you, you look like the kind of girl who would strip on top of a giant concrete structure in the middle of a graveyard?"

Few things in life sound as good to Lenny as the sound of a bottle of beer opening. He grabs one and heads to his recliner to catch up on some shitty reality TV he DVR'd last night. He cracks the can and lets the foam roll over his hand and drip into his lap. He sips it up and inhales the sweet taste of inebriation.

As soon as his ass touches the cushion his phone starts ringing. Caller ID reveals it's Stanley Kane's office.

"Jesus Christ," he says to himself while rolling his eyes. "Yeah, hey Stanley. How's it going?"

"Hi, Lenny!" It's Ms. Barbeau.

Lenny thinks she's the type of girl who would fight off an ancient genie in a bowling alley. She's a total babe, but also Kane's right-hand woman. She would sell out her own mom if it meant she could get a part acting in the *Robot Ninja* series. He remembers when she asked him on a date last year and spent the whole time trying to convince Lenny to create a sidekick for Robot Ninja called Robot Neena that was based on her appearance. Lenny could think of worse ideas—and he was about to hear some.

"Hi, Ms. Barbeau. How are you doing?"

"I'm doing… GREAT! Unlike YOU, Lenny. I'm sorry to call you but it looks like you made Mr. Kane downright upset with the new issue of *Robot Ninja*. It doesn't look ANYTHING like the TV show. What's with that?"

"Ms. Barbeau, you're the kind of woman who would be nearly scared to death in a barn by a monster in a bad sequel to a great movie. Just let me talk to Stanley."

Lenny looks at his beer longingly while he listens to a muzak version of a Dead Kennedy's song.

Who makes this shit?

Probably some guy named Adam.

He watches the beer like it's a new Meghan Trainor video and he can't break his eyes away.

"Goddamnit, hurry up Stanley," he says to himself.

"Leonard?"

About damn time.

"Hey, Kane. Get to it. What's the issue?"

"This new *Robot Ninja*. It's…"

"Amazing? Incredible? A sad and accurate reflection of our modern society?"

"SHIT! It's shit, Leonard!"

"Couldn't help but notice you didn't put 'the' before 'shit'."

"Listen very closely. The only word I would even consider putting before 'shit' in that sentence would be 'dog,' or maybe even 'cat'. But definitely not 'the.' This thing is nothing like the show! I thought we agreed the new issues would be a straight adaptation."

"Oh. for fuck's sake. I told you all. I talked to my agent; we all had an agreement. You and everyone else can fuck up the show as bad as you want, but the comic is mine. I'm not going to give my readers a watered-down version of Robert Pattinson as Batman. And I'm not writing any of that Marvel movie style shit. My readers expect…"

"I don't give a flying anaconda! That 'shit' sells, Leonard! It fucking SELLS! Look at the merchandising check you got last month. Go look at what's trending. Can't we agree to maybe do a one-off graphic novel."

"Listen, either you print the comic I sent, or I won't write another page. I'll fucking quit."

"I'll print it, goddamnit. But you listen to me, when your contract is up, we're going to have a serious conversation. I just had a wonderful artist in here, his hands are insured for ten thousand bucks! He wants to do a new swamp monster story-"

Lenny doesn't hear the rest because he hangs up. Somewhere miles away, Stanley Kane is saying, "Damn artists…" and shaking his head at the same time Lenny says, "Damn publishers…"

The program he recorded caught a little bit of the local news beforehand, usually not a big deal; sometimes a news anchor accidentally says something really stupid and gets canned. Not this time, this time the recording started in the middle of a story about two people who were brutally killed the night before after a nice dinner date.

The news anchor rattles on about the diabolical nature of the crime; she says the poor woman's mother heard a rumor her boyfriend was going to propose that night.

"The Ridgeway Murders."

That's what they called this incident, and others like it from before.

He turns off the TV. His beer slightly spilling to the floor as he leans forward in shock.

He realizes and places it on the table before putting his hands over his face.

"Goddamnit," he says to himself. He can feel all the emotions again like a raw exposed nerve being fiddled with by the world's worst dentist. He closes his eyes and cringes, the emotional memories taking on a nearly physical pain.

He can feel the solution; he knows what he has to do. Someone has to do something about this shit. People can't just kill people in his town. People can't just steal your life's work and make a cheap buck off it.

He looks at the poster hanging on the far wall. It's a blown-up image of the first cover for *Robot Ninja*. He nods his head.

Leonard Miller created *Robot Ninja* to stop this kind of injustice. Maybe now it's time for Leonard Miller to become Robot Ninja.

8

***

In the same way Leonard Miller enjoys a beer after meeting with his asshole publisher, Dr. Goodknight enjoys playing some VR after a long day of trying to invent the next best product to sell at department stores with an "As seen on TV" sticker slapped on the box. He always plugs in a modification for his samurai game that allows him to hack and slash through a department store. He would show those fuckers the right way to move up and down aisles... virtually. Nothing, NOTHING, pissed Goodknight off more than when people traveled the wrong way down the aisle while shopping. Despite some assholes' opinions, there IS a right and wrong way to go up and down a shopping aisle. You follow the rules of the road. The people who don't are the same kind of people that think they can say any offensive and derogatory thing, then when someone is mad, they say, "Sorry you don't have thick enough skin. I'm an asshole, deal with it." The kind of people who think everyone should adjust to their behavior. They also probably don't take the carts back to the corral... fucking losers.

It's been twenty years since he invented the all-in-one hot dog cooker; a toaster style item that cooks your dogs in the middle and grills your buns on the sides. This is an event that added to his hate of supercenters. He spent so much time in them advertising the machine that he became hyper-fixated on the rudeness of others present in these stores. He hadn't had to go in one for a while thanks to home delivery.

With the recent surge in services that deliver food from anywhere, he's noticed a dramatic drop off in his checks. It seems like people are getting their dogs delivered instead of cooking them at home. Maybe the stores don't have the device in good enough spots? Then again, hot dog delivery was really damn cool.

It was a good run while it lasted.

Not too bad for a man who started off creating some of the deadliest weapons known to man for the Army (including a biological disease that seemingly made the dead live again).

He could have made big money from that one if his partner hadn't run off and hid in a basement somewhere.

He looks at the script the ad company sent him. The Glizzy Gladiator. That's who they wanted him to be. "Play into the memes!" the guy said. *What the hell is a glizzy?* Goodknight thought. He would have never guessed that a world-renowned weapons designer would be so involved in the lucrative market of tubed processed meat.

He started to long for the days of making weapons. His life had some meaning then. He was protecting the American people, goddamnit! He was making guns and bombs that would roast the asses of anyone who dared to challenge the freedoms of the red, white, and goddamned blue. It was fulfilling. Every time he looked into the eyes of his wife and son, he would think about how his products saved them daily.

Until they didn't.

It had been a quiet night penetrated by the sound of an explosion and body parts flying into walls. He ran from his office into his son's bedroom where he found his wife and kid splattered all over the walls, thanks to his newest invention. How did the boy get it? How did he know what button to push? These are the thoughts that keep Goodknight from sleeping and drove him into the food industry.

He needed something more than trying to invent new ways to cook crummy food. *Christ,* he thinks, *why didn't I invent the microwave?* He tries to think of a new invention that can cook his son's favorite food, pizza. His brain starts to hurt as the idea of pepperoni mixes with the pixelated gore pumping into his headset.

Gore that looks suspiciously like...

He trails off in his thoughts as he hacks and slashes his way through enemies attacking him in his VR game. He swings the sword back and forth through the air. He swings his plastic controller hard through the air at the next wave of assassins.

Thud.

"Ow!"

He takes off his head set and there's Leonard.

"Leonard!" he says. "Don't sneak up on a man with a sword!"

"I'm sorry Dr. Goodknight, but I need your help in a bad way."

"What is it? I'm playing *Warriors of the Rising Sun?*"

"You've got to help. I have a great idea. I need a suit. Like this."

Goodknight looks at the poster Leonard has unrolled in front of him.

"You want to be Robot Ninja?" he asks.

"Who better to fight crime around here. You know, like the people who killed that couple the other night. That bitch that kicked my ass. I think the costume will be enough to freak them out, or at least keep them busy long enough to call the cops. How do you think Batman got so good?"

"Yes, but Batman was also a very rich man in his alter ego."

Leonard drops a wad of hundreds on the table and says, "Don't worry about that, I just got my royalties from that dog AND cat shit TV show."

"Leonard, I'm an inventor. Not a costume maker."

But Goodknight studies the picture for a minute. This could be it. This could be the break he needs. He thinks to himself about how nice it would be to contribute something to the world again (other than cooked processed meat tubes). If he couldn't protect his actual son with his inventions, maybe he could...

"Alright, Leonard," he says. "I'll do it for you."

"Yes! Thanks, Doc! I'm outta here. I gotta go train."

Leonard punches the air a few times like a boxer on his way out.

"Hey, Leonard," Goodknight says.

"Yeah?"

"What's a glizzy?"

9

Something is in the air, shifting like a fog or haze. It stays the same in genetic build up but shifts in shape. It's a vision that is morphing from detachment and escapism, into personal loss and gain. Lenny's mind has decided to blur the line between reality and make believe. His brain works to convince him that he's been the one having these adventures in a robot suit. He starts to fall for the trickery of his own mind, but instead he shakes head back and forth, dislodging the slippery little claws that have embedded themselves into his logic. A simple logic that says: *Lenny, you are not a comic character.*

He decides to do what he's always done: draw. Whenever he needs peace and quiet from the noise his brain is making, he's always used drawing. He can stop the worst spiral of depression within himself by creating. He goes to his desk and sits down with his supplies that act as the medical equipment saving his life.

The pencil waves across the page creating the images from Lenny's head like a magic wand. The couple will survive this time. They will live, have kids, get their dream jobs, have grandchildren; their kids will have dream jobs, their grandkids will save the world from the pollution of man. In a way, Robot Ninja will do all of these things. If Robot Ninja doesn't save them, their great grandkids won't be able to create a pig and spider hybrid that shoots webs of bacon instead of silk.

Lenny always had an image in his head of what Robot Ninja's human face would look like. He always dream cast an actor like Dan Stevens in the costume. As he drew panel after panel, he began to notice something...

A panel with twin blades piercing through the woman's eye sockets.

A panel with the driver trying to remove his severed foot from his own ass.

The other man chewing on a frozen dog turd until Robot Ninja's foot stomps on the back of his head and sends the turd-sicle through the back of his skull.

A panel that was a closeup of Robot Ninja's face; half robot and the other half showing the face of the man who died so Robot Ninja could live. One half machine, the other looking vaguely like Lenny...

"Oh, fuck yeah," Lenny says to himself. "Lenny Miller, Robot mother fucking Ninja."

He leans his head back and looks around his bedroom for inspiration and sees a poster of a medieval battle. A man is swinging a massive club with a spiked ball attached to it by chain.

Lenny draws a cannon on Robot Ninja's arm. He takes a picture and sends it to Dr. Goodknight with a text that says, *"Can you do this? Like MegaMan?"*

10

I knew I should have come here, Dr. Goodknight thinks. His stomach is grumbling for some food, and he can't find the right size screw he needs to make this damn canon. Why not tell Leonard it's not possible? Because he wants to build the damn thing and he has to go to another store now anyway because he's craving fried cheese.

AT the hardware store, he picks up sandpaper and loads it into his basket. Nuts and bolts, chunks of metal that can be sanded and welded into blades with the ability to slice through a goddamn T-Rex skull.

He sets his basket on the counter. The clerk at the register looks him up and down.

"I'm building a suit for a friend," Goodknight says. "He wants to be a real-life transformer."

The clerk starts ringing him up with a curious look.

"Is this some sort of video sketch?" the clerk asks.

"Ok, you figured us out. My camera man is right there." Goodknight points at a random guy; the guy is trying to decide between two hammers. "Darn, guess I'll just pay and leave. No reaction from you, huh, smart guy?"

Goodknight loads his stuff into his trunk. The hammer

debater comes out carrying a hammer with a green handle. It's neither of the two that he was undecided about.

Goodknight drives across town to the local Walmart. He makes his way to the deli and buys some fried cheese to eat while he shops for everything else he needs.

"Didjya pay for those?" asks a man in a flannel.

"Yes," says Goodknight.

"Well, I'm making sure because they ring them up by weight."

"Ok. I paid for them. And isn't that why the barcode is on it?"

"I'm just saying, that could be considered theft if you didn't pay for them?"

"And who the hell are you anyway? Sam fucking Walton's long-lost nephew? Do you want to see my receipt? Goddamn the monotony of life."

"You may not like the money of life, but you still gotta pay for it. I'm just a concerned citizen."

"I said monotony. This everyday trivial stuff you're making me go through. Concern yourself with kissing my ass. Here."

Goodknight hands him the receipt and leaves the aisle in a tantrum.

He smashes his cart into a woman who's pushing her cart the wrong way down the aisle.

"Does no one know that you push a cart like you drive? Are you British? Get in the right lane, lady!"

"I'm… sorry?"

Goodknight doesn't respond; he's already scooping shit and slamming it in his cart.

He gets to the self-checkout and starts ringing stuff up as fast as he can. The belt sander won't fit into a bag, so he leaves it unbagged.

Big mistake.

He regrets every second of that.

As he heads out the door, he's stopped by an elderly gentleman who says, "Sir, I'm sorry to bother you, but new store policy is to check any unbagged item is on the receipt."

Goodknight hands the man the receipt. He scans down it looking for the belt sander all while Goodknight stands there tapping his foot and saying, "The goddamned monotony of life."

"Oh! There it is. Have a good day."

Goodknight nods and practically runs out the door. He feels bad about his attitude, but he'll be damned if that store doesn't make even a patient man like himself into a crazy person. He crosses the road and a car honks at him.

He didn't look both ways, this was totally his fault, but instead of apologizing he stares at the man with lasers coming from his eyes.

He gets in his car and sighs; he doesn't like the person mass-consumerism turns him into in moments like these.

He shakes his head and signs an invisible contract with himself to donate some money to charity or something.

When he gets home, he heads straight to the garage and starts working.

He hangs a steak from the ceiling and slices it as easy as a hot knife through butter with the talons he's made.

He shoots the chest pad with a small handgun and brushes off the residue. Not even a scratch.

Now comes the big test. The hand canon.

He loads it with a hollow glass ball he's designed to shatter when being fired; the glass shards will shoot out as fast as a bullet.

He pulls the trigger and watches as the whole turkey he bought is sliced up worse than if a toddler was cutting it for Thanksgiving. Meat falls in ribbons to floor; the bones are cleanly cut.

He nods and places another turkey in its spot.

This time he loads the hand cannon with a metal ball covered in tiny spikes.

When he pulls the trigger, the turkey explodes sending meat and bone everywhere.

This is really going to rock someone's world, he thinks as he cleans up.

He's back upstairs watching a TikTok where this guy has constructed a giant metal pad and spring into some handheld contraption that pushes a solid square of steel forward with the force of a Mike Tyson punch.

When the pizza guy shows up, he shows him the video and asks, "You think this would hurt?"

"Uhhhhh, I think it would fucking kill someone, bro."

He tips the guy a fifty.

As he's eating, he texts Leonard, *"Wait until you see what I've built."*

11

Lenny can't shake that feeling of needing to go, needing to move. He drew for two hours but his wrist started to kill him; his hand was cramping. He lay down on the ground and tried to meditate but all he could think about was the injustice that had been done to him. *How can someone take something that means so much to someone and use it as a way to make a cheap profit? How in the fuck does one person sell another's soul?*

Let's face it, that's what happened. Lenny invested his heart and soul into creating a character and some shit bag TV exec took it from him. He struggles to even think of Robot Ninja as his character alone now. It's like Robot Ninja is the child of an ugly divorce now; he has to live two seperate lives. It isn't fair. Lenny uses this excess emotional energy as fuel to exercise.

Fucking assholes.

Every time Lenny gets to the top of his sit-up, he thinks this and punches the air.

He feels betrayed.

How the fuck can his publisher just say, "Oh, by the way there's a new artist in town!"

No there isn't.

At least not one who will work as cheaply as Lenny did for so many years.

That's the thing no one wants to think about right now. When that place was just a little muddy shithole on 7th Street, just starting, Lenny Miller, the man who left one of the big two, he came walking in and said, "Alright, I need an independent place to let me do this. These Captain America fucks won't let me."

He took a massive pay cut that day.

50/50 royalties from an unknown publisher doesn't even halfway compare to 20/80 from his previous publisher.

He worked his ass off.

Promo tours.

Finding other pissed off artists.

He pulled that place up from poverty with *Robot Ninja.*

Now they want to kick him to the curb because some new asshole can draw a swamp monster?

Go fuck yourself.

How many other artists have tried to overthrow him? Countless. Lenny always manages to survive the onslaught of badly ripped-off Marvel or DC comics. One time he had someone try to pitch Robot Ninja vs Spawn. Guy said he knew McFarland and everything. He's outlived the stupid shit and brought *Robot Ninja* with him. That mechanical creation who learned karate on a rooftop somewhere in Los Angeles went from a negative profit, to now having a fast-food chain releasing special souvenir cups to coincide with the TV show. Which is worse? Being so poor you can't own anything but your dignity and stubbornness, or being well-off enough that you can afford to buy the long out of print novelization of your comic book online at fifteen times retail?

There's always someone trying to take Lenny's spot in comics; and why not? Lenny made it here on sheer determination, so why couldn't someone else?

Because someone else is trying to destroy me, not work side-by-side.

Lenny wouldn't mind a partner. He has often longed for someone to step up and create something that could exist alongside Robot Ninja. Batman has Robin, Aquaman has Aqualad, where is Robot Ninja's equal? Where is Lenny Miller's equal?

He should stop by the comic office in his new gear when he gets it, really show those people what he's done for them. Then, they'll have to apologize and appreciate him. If he did that they'd have to say, "Wow, this is truly the goddamned Robot Ninja. Sorry we ever had the audacity to doubt you, Lenny."

Lenny stands up and bends over his drawing desk. He looks at his last drawing, one he knows they won't like because they can't do it on the TV show. Anything that can be done on TV is chicken shit by nature.

All of this, and STILL he does the comic by himself. STILL he cannot afford anything but a three-room apartment; one of those rooms is a bathroom even! He had always thought the amount of money he was making was great, all the way up until he realized the pay he got in royalties for each back issue was barely enough to buy the issue itself! He thinks to himself about how Amsteel should pay him what he's worth and give him some respect.

"Fat fucking chance of that," he says. "The only thing they appreciate about me is the cash, the dollars, the checks."

His phone buzzes with a call from Goodknight.

It's ready…

12
____

In the mirror stands a figure in all black with a red belt tied around his waist. He's wearing a silver mask that covers his face, with a red visor for vision. Lenny stretches and looks at himself. He holds the talons up in the air and pretends to swipe them across someone's throat.

This is so bad ass, he thinks as he leaves the bathroom.

He stalks through Goodknight's house pretending to infiltrate an enemy compound. He looks in every room before moving down the hallway. He sees everything as a threat to the goodness of humanity until it proves itself otherwise. Everyone and everything is capable of evil; let them decide which they want to be.

"Here I come," Lenny says as he walks through the doorway in complete Robot Ninja costume. He pauses in the doorway and watches as Goodknight yawns. _The man has been going for hours,_ Lenny thinks. _Probably took some of those crazy ass pills he invented that made soldiers stay awake for two weeks straight._

Lenny remembers the stories about that one. The soldiers that stayed awake so long that they started hallucinating and seeing each other as aliens. The training compound turned into some fucked up version of a video game.

Goodknight still pops one every now and again when he

needs a night awake. He told Lenny he perfected it down to a 24-hour period per capsule.

"Well," Lenny says, "how do I look?"

Goodknight stretches back and gives Lenny a quick nod of his head. "There is one more feature I need to show you," Goodknight says.

He walks to Lenny and flips a switch on the side of the mask.

"Go ahead, say something," Goodknight says. "Go on, anything."

"What, Goodknight?" Lenny says. His voice startled him. It sounds like one of the robots from that CGI movie about cars turning into humanoid machines. "Shit, this is amazing! Hold it right there, scum!"

"It's a voice changer. One of the tech companies I work with wanted me to design it. Something about helping the AI sound like other people. This one is just a prototype. But it should suffice for your needs."

"This is great. How can I lose with all of this shit on my side?"

"Be careful, Lenny."

"I feel invincible!"

"Yeah well, let's hope so."

Goodknight's alarm goes off. He set the thing up to let him know when he needs to go to bed to get eight and a half hours of sleep. A sort of reverse alarm.

Lenny pats Goodknight on the back; he can tell his friend is exhausted. "You went to Walmart, didn't you?" Lenny asks.

"Yeah," Goodknight says. "That place. The people in it. Anarchy. Total and complete anarchy. I better go get some rest."

"You do that. I know how that place takes it out of you. I'm heading out on patrol."

"You're going out tonight?"

"Yeah! How else am I going to catch these dickheads in the act?"

"I really think you should get some sleep."

"I'm used to no sleep. That's how I get comics done so fast."

"Alright, well, please be careful, and come back tomorrow. I have some other stuff to show you. Goodknight, Leonard."

"Good night, Goodknight."

"Ha. Very funny."

Lenny watches for the upstairs door to close. When he sees the light from the kitchen enter the stairwell, and then the door closing and blocking it out, he heads over to the medicine cabinet.

There they are, the pills.

Lenny pops the top off and crams five or more in his mouth. He's going to need the energy.

As soon as he swallows the first one, the ache in his arm from drawing vanishes. His eyes feel as if they are frozen open. He tries to close his eyelids for a bit but only finds himself frustrated. He knows this shit is going to work. He'll be awake forever.

13

Stuart always volunteers for the extra shifts at work. Easy money. No one ever comes into a video store to rent DVDs anymore; usually it's just babes coming in to use the tanning beds. Ever since the end of the video rental era, these stores transitioned into tanning places that just happened to still have some movies to rent. Not that the babes are a bad part of the job; Stuart thinks it may be the best part of the whole gig. One time, this babe totally forgot to get dressed before she came back out into the store. That was a good day. The only days that compare are when he gets to watch movies all day and night.

His new bootleg Meghan Trainor concert DVD arrived in the mail, and he was stressed about getting to use the big TV at home to watch it. His mom was always watching some shitty reruns of some shitty show. Usually, *The King of Queens* or similar ick. He wished he was working tonight; that would solve the problem.

The text came through from his coworker, Candy, that she needed the night off on very short notice and he jumped at the chance. He could use the giant sixty-five incher to watch the DVD. He never liked Candy, but tonight she was his favorite coworker.

He was singing along, all by himself. The tune was *Title*; Meghan was in the crowd playing a ukulele while she sang it.

A true icon.

He caught a van parking in the lot out of the corner of his eyes. Three people dressed in worn out clothes and sporting bandanas get out.

Now Stu, he thinks, *don't be judgmental. These people may just be looking for the new Spider-Man movie.*

The door flies open, the force almost shattering the glass as it hits the wall. The woman of the group walks in front of the TV and pushes the power button. She turns to look at Stu and says, "I hate that bass bitch."

The two guys with her laugh.

The group looks around the video store. They pull DVDs and Blu Rays off the shelves and laugh at some inside joke about each one.

They walk up to the counter and the woman asks, "Do y'all got the new Spider-Man movie?"

Stuart tells them that unfortunately it was rented earlier in the day.

Two knives and a gun are suddenly pointed at him.

The woman says, "In that case, we'll take all the money in the register."

Stuart pops the drawer and holds out the fifty that's in there.

"Fifty? You fucking kidding me? You want to die?"

"I'm sorry, most people either pay with a card, or online when they schedule. I'm sort of just an overhyped door man."

"Hey, Gody," says Revelle. "My Spidey sense is tingling and telling me we need to fucking waste this guy!"

"Shut the fuck up, Revelle. Scully, is that a car outside?"

"Sure is, sure is. Looks like some rich bitch and her little brother. Easy pickin's."

Gody nods and they all move into the aisles and wait.

"Goddamn soup stain," Officer Hickox mumbles to himself as he brushes his shirt. His son has been on a kick with trying new Pinterest recipe ideas. At eight-years-old, the little guy acts like he's the next Gordon Ramsey.

Last night the kid whipped up some shrimp and clams, all fresh of course, boiled in a nice ale, with a side of grilled brioche. Hickox and his wife sat at the kitchen table while their son put raw onion in a pan with some butter and fresh garlic to create a base. Then he poured two bottles of beer into the mix and brought it to a boil. When they had the food, the broth was perfect for soaking the bread. The bitter taste of the beer mixed with the grilled butter on the bread was heavenly.

The biggest issue was that Hickox couldn't focus for shit. All he could think about was that poor dead couple he didn't get to in time. He hoped the guy who did get there and caught a hand full of ass whooping for his troubles, was ok.

This place was going to shit. He had been tracking the gang for close to two months; now he finally has one of the leaders in his mind. Whoever that guy was, he did Hickox a huge favor.

He ran the plates as the van fled that night and discovered it was registered to a man named Revelle (shitty name for a guy).

He did some research and found out that Revelle spent quite a lot of time with a woman named Gody. The same Gody that he's had to take to jail for violent behavior around ten times prior. Fucking higher-ups wouldn't do anything except say, "She's had a hard life."

How many second chances does a person get? Apparently as many as they like. If it were up to him, this woman would have been locked away forever the first time they had her. You look in her eyes and you can tell she doesn't hate pain or violence; she loves both. She loves them like the twin sons she never had. Hickox can see murderous pleasure in her eyes.

He feels a chill go down his spine. What is he doing here without backup? He knows she'll show up with her whole gang. He found the third member's personal blog site last Thursday. *Movies with the crew tonight,*" said today's post. He knew where they were going, so he went.

Now, here he sits, in his patrol car. Driving around with a pierogi soup stain on his shirt and an emotional stain on his heart.

He pulls up to a stop light and sits, the thoughts weighing on his mind.

What I would give to see that white van again, he thinks.

And there, in the parking lot of the tanning place, the last video store he had to check, sits the van…

15

Christina Moulton sat by the phone anxiously waiting for George to call. *Why in the world did we have to move to a place with no cell service?* she thinks. If her parents would just spring for Wi-Fi, she could use that for calls. But nooooooo they want her to waste her teenage years sitting beside a landline phone or at the library doing online schoolwork.

The only good thing about this is that she was finding more time for reading. She recently picked up an anthology of the best new comic books; it was a whim, but now she was in love. The heroes all had these specific traits she related to. She wanted to, needed to, tell George about it.

She picks up the handset to make sure it's connected. She hears her mother's voice saying, "...to the casino! Can you believe it? That's nowhere for a five year..."

"MOM! I'm waiting on George to call! You know that!"

"Sorry, honey. Hey, do me a favor: take your brother into town and drop off those movies we got. Thanks! I'll tell George you'll be back soon."

Movies! DVDs! Why can't these cheap-o's just spring for Wi-Fi? Then they could stream whatever they wanted, and no one would have to make a perilous journey across town at night. She shakes her head because she knows her little brother Christopher will be excited about the trip. He's kind of gotten a weird little obsession with the movie store. He always rents two or three movies at a time. Watching him browse the aisles is as close to torture as Christina ever wants to get. The last time he picked up *Good Will Hunting*, carried it for an hour, then set it down because it actually sounded lame, and picked up some dragon movie called *Reign of Fire*. She had to admit it now though, the dragon movie kind of ruled.

She hangs up the phone and yells for Christopher. As they pass their father on his recliner he asks, "Hey, Chris, where you off to?"

The siblings answer in unison, "Taking movies back."

Christina shudders in anger.

Why are her parents so dumb they named them both something that can be shortened to Chris?

"Did you like that new The Rock movie, Chris?"

"Dad," says Christina. "Neither one of us know who you're talking to. And that wasn't The Rock. That was Vin Diesel. And the movie is hella old."

"Oh, I thought The Rock played that Red Dick guy."

"RIDDICK, DAD! RIDDICK!"

Christina storms out of the front door leaving Christopher alone.

Just another day at the Moulton residence.

"For what it's worth, dad," Christopher says. "I liked the movie."

The siblings drive across town in silence. Both Chris's are tired of trying to bond over anything other than how annoying their parents are. Christina turns on the radio; it's playing Meghan Trainor. She sighs and turns it off saying, "People who listen to that should be shot."

Christina whips her father's BMW into the movie store parking lot and says, "Tell Stuart I'll be here for my morning tan and give him this." She hands Christopher a twenty. "Now hurry up, George will be calling any minute!"

"Alright! God! It's not my fault mom forgot to bring them back."

As Christopher walks across the parking lot, Christina wishes she was an only child.

16

Lenny saw the van as he drove by the video store. The side door was wide open, so he slipped out of his car and into the van. He slides the door shut and waits for the big birthday surprise.

He hears a gunshot from inside the video store and clenches his fist. *Goddamnit!* he thinks. *I may be too late. Why can't I just go in and take care of this? The element of surprise is so important though.*

The three assholes from the other night come pouring out of the video store. Revelle has his arm locked around a kid's throat and Sculley is talking about wasting the store clerk and reenacting the scene. He shoots finger guns into the air and yells bang.

No! thinks Lenny, *Stuart?*

The crew rips a young woman from a car and drag her toward the van. They're going to pull off another kidnapping today if he can't stop them.

He will stop them this time.

The door slides open fast, and Lenny jumps out. He points the twin talons on his hand at Sculley.

"Hey, you goofy fucker," says Gody. "Cut the Halloween shit and beat it or…" she snatches the kid from Revelle, "I'll fucking kill this kid."

Revelle takes this chance and moves in on the older sister.

The kid yells, "Christina!"

The kid's sister yells "Christopher!"

Lenny thinks it's odd that they both have names that could be shortened to Chris but doesn't spend too much time worrying about it. Revelle has thrown Christina onto the floor of the van and ripped her top in half.

"Show me them huge knockers!" Revelle yells as he reaches for her bra.

Lenny kicks him hard in the stomach.

Gody screams out and tosses Christopher away.

The kid's head hits the ground and makes a thud like a pineapple hitting a concrete wall.

"Leave him alone, mother fucker!" yells Gody as she points her gun on Lenny.

"Who the fuck are you?" Revelle asks.

"I'm Robot Ninja," Lenny says. "And I kick ass."

Lenny stabs Revelle in the chest with the steel talons and shoves him against the van. He can feel and hear the sound of metal scraping against rib bones. He knows the pain has to be unbearable. He pulls his arm back and punches them through the man's eye sockets. It feels like stabbing a grape. The talons get stuck in the bone and Lenny moves them in and out like his looking for a violent and gory orgasm. In-out-in-out. Blood flows from the wound as the man's body slowly falls down. Brain matter that looks like sliced steak pours from the empty eye socket.

Gody shoots at Lenny and blows out the window of the van.

The lights of a cop car illuminate the night.

Lenny runs as fast as he can back to his hidden car. He looks over his shoulder and sees the van peeling out across the concrete pavement.

A police officer who Lenny knows, Officer Hickox, gets out and runs to the kids who could both go by Chris.

Lenny starts his car and casually drives by as if he's passing traffic. The girl is crying and holding her brother's bloody head.

Lenny sees Revelle's dead body and whispers to himself, "I did it."

17

Lucid dreaming is a crazy thing. You lay there, completely awake, but also completely asleep. You're able to manipulate the world around you and bend the rules of the dreamworld.

Lenny is somewhere between lucid dreaming and a bad acid trip as he lay in bed tossing and turning. He an't sleep (because of all the pep pills he'd taken at Goodnight's), but his body won't stay awake. He rolls one way and another the whole night. The sound of the little boy's head hitting the concrete playing over and over again in his head like a drumbeat.

Bum-bum tish.

Bum-bum tish.

He sees the blades going in and out of the criminal's skull. The scene changes to a dick and vagina. The scene morphs again to claws and eye sockets. Maybe it all was slightly orgasmic.

He finally gives up and throws the blankets off himself when he hears someone banging on his apartment door. Surely, the cops haven't figured him out yet?

He opens the door to Doctor Goodknight. He's holding a newspaper in Lenny's face. "Have some fun last night," he says storming into the apartment. "You killed that boy, Leonard. You killed him."

"Good morning, Goodknight," says Lenny. "He was a scum-bag; he deserved what he got. You should have seen the way those blades sliced through his skull."

"Not him, you idiot. The kid, the child. Look."

Lenny sits down in his recliner and reads out loud: *"Last night three victims were found, Stuart Ranshow, Revelle Rodd, and... Jesus Christ."*

"No, Leonard. It wasn't Jesus. It's your fault that child is dead."

"No, that woman, she was the leader. It's her fault."

"If you hadn't been there, it wouldn't have happened."

"Whatever, Goodknight. You didn't see how they behaved. That kid was as good as dead anyway. At least I saved his sister."

"Where's the costume, Lenny. No more, you're not going out again. No way."

"I have to. I have to stop that woman. She's making the world miserable. Just like my agent and publisher."

"Is that what this is all about? Your little comic? There are real lives at stake here, Leonard."

Goodknight grabs Lenny's arm. Lenny shoves him hard against the wall. Goodknight's body leaves a Doc-shaped dent in the plywood wall of the apartment. The physical pain is nothing compared to the emotional pain Goodknight is feeling in the moment. He wants to fight back; he wants to kill Lenny before Lenny can kill him—or someone else. Instead, he does the same thing so many of us who sense danger do. He does nothing.

"I see," says Goodknight. "It looks like my uppers you stole still have their super strength side effects when you take too many."

"Fuck you, Goodknight."

"Tell it to the cops, Leonard."

Lenny watches the door slam.

Goodknight and shakes his head.

Lenny knows he's really made a mess of shit. But, as soon as he takes out the leader of that gang, it will all be ok.

18

Lenny has been stalking that black van for four hours. He's circled them using alleyways, tailing them so close he could hit their bumper. The gang must be planning something big because they've picked up around five other guys, making seven total in the van.

Seven dead criminal fucks.

Seven dead publishers.

Seven dead agents.

Lenny shakes the confusion from his mind.

I'm doing this for the world, he thinks. *Not for my comic.*

The van turns down an alleyway and parks at the back entrance of a bank. Lenny can see a cleaning lady running a vacuum through the glass door.

He whips his car in front of the van and climbs out of the driver's seat. He gets into a fighting stance in the alley and prepares for the war he knows is coming.

"This fucking robo dick again?" says Gody. "Fuck him up! I want his heart covered in gravel under my shoe!"

Five goons approache Lenny as Sculley stays with Gody, taking in the oncoming violence.

Lenny slashes out with his talons and catches one of the men in the shoulder. His blades slice through skin and lodge into bone. But the time it takes for him to get the claws back out is all it takes for him to be knocked to the ground and pinned down by the four others.

He feels a barrage of punches and kicks all over his body.

One man kneels beside him and punches him hard in the chest; he feels a rib start to crack.

"This one's for Revelle, mother fucker!" the man yells as he pummels Lenny's chest. Lenny throws his arm out to block and slices the guy's hand completely off. Blood shoots out of the end covering the other four like a hose.

"Holy fucking hell!" yells Gody. "Hold his ass down!"

Gody and Sculley join the gang and throw some kicks into Lenny's ribs for good measure. Sculley puts all of his weight on Lenny's right arm, pinning it to the ground. Lenny can feel the imprint on the underside of the boot.

"Let's see if a robot ninja can bleed," says Gody as she pulls out a pocketknife. She cuts away the fabric on Lenny's wrist and drives the knife deep. She slowly pulls it toward her, cutting through layers of skin.

Lenny cries out in pain as he feels tendons being severed.

Gody stands up after the damage is done and begins kicking Lenny in the face. Lenny can feel the mask bending and denting into his flesh. The visor cracks and a piece of glass stabs him beside his right eye.

"Get this dickhead to the van," Gody says. "Let's take him home and have some fun."

As the crew is carrying Lenny, the red and blue lights of a police car illuminate the alleyway. Lenny glances and sees the cleaning lady in the doorway on her phone. He uses the distraction to kick Sculley's foot out. He plants his heel square on the middle of Sculley's sensitive balls. The crew, now off balanced and distracted, drop Lenny.

"My nuts!" Sculley yells as he shuffles to his car.

Lenny hears gunfire and feels a punch in his back. As he's falling, his shoulder explodes like a water balloon filled with meat and blood. He turns and sees Gody holding a gun and grinning. She then points it at the police officers.

He drops down into the driver's seat and peels the mask from his face so he can see. His nose has become so swollen that he has to pry it out of the mask. It was lodged in there so tight he could feel himself not being able to breathe.

He turns on his car and takes off through the crisscrossing gunfire.

He sees a man's stomach explode from a bullet as he's passing; the man struggles to hold his insides in as they fall to the concrete.

Lenny escapes the alleyway and begins to softly sob. Is this truly what he wanted? This pain? This violence? What is all of this? Is a violence so violent even helping his cause?

He knows the only person who can help him now is Dr. Goodknight.

19

Lenny stumbles from his car. His legs feel like they're made of melting candle wax and he can't seem to convince his mind that they aren't. *Is this how I go?* he asks himself in his mind. Do I melt away like a candle left to burn too long with no cool down time at all. It feels like his whole body is turning into a melted slop on the cold concrete. His mind pictures a pile of gore mixed with wires and electronic devices. *Robot Ninja pudding, mother fuckers,* he thinks as his foot slips into a doorway.

He fucks around with his new perception of reality and pretends to roll down the stairs like some sort of gelatinous melted meat skin fucker. He ends up sliding down a few stairs on his feet before landing on his ass.

"What if the ass was a whole bone?" His question sends him into a laughing fit as he flows like lava down into the basement. The puddle that is Lenny Miller gets back on two feet and sobers up instantly when he sees what is on the TV.

News reporter says, "I feel so bad for what happened here today. But we have an eyewitness who was there. Sir, tell us what you saw, what happened?"

"Oh, hey, shout out mom! What up Aunt Linda! Breanna! You

know you're my number one, my only girl. Hey, Eric, Nikki why don't y'all get the grill out..."

"SIR! This isn't *The Price is Right*. This is live TV. Can you PLEASE tell us what you saw."

"Oh, yeah, sure. This guy, probably six-one, right? He's all decked out in black. He's got this red sash tied around his waist like he just left Karate class. He was wearing this silver mask that kind of looked like a bent plate. It had this red visor going across the eyes. He sorta looked badass, but then I noticed he was wearing slippers. Slippers! Wouldn't they get wet and like become a fungal nightmare between his toes? It also seems kind of silly..."

"BUT WHAT HAPPENED? What did you see happen? What did he do?"

"Oh... I didn't see anything."

"Back to you, studio."

Lenny couldn't tell if the reporter's eye was twitching from anger or if it was the swelling of his own eye making the TV twitch, so he punches a hole in the screen for good measure. No one else is fucking with Robot Miller tonight.

"GOODKNIGHT!" he yells. "GOODKNIGHT, PLEASE HELP!"

He remembered when the doctor told him he slept with noise canceling headphones sometimes. *Great decision Doc*, Lenny thinks. *I'm in your basement, what if I were a murderer?*

He sits at Goodknight's workstation and takes a survey of his arm. It looks like it is made of strawberry ice cream, and someone scooped a chunk out. A gaping hole covered in raw meat, blood, severed tendons, and muscle stares at him like the Grand Canyon. He can't feel any pain thanks to the Doc's special formula, but he can tell this isn't good. He sticks his finger in the wound and spreads it open, surveying the damage. He can see his bone poking out through some muscle. He cuts two plastic tubes and pinches his blood vessels with his fingers. He takes one of the tubes and jams it into one of the spots where the blood is running most, and into the matching spot on the other side of the wound. He does the same with the other tube. He grabs a piece of metal and wraps it around the tubes, then he forces it deeper into the wound to connect the tubes to his bone for support. He wraps the whole thing in duct tape.

When he tries to stand, he notices his left leg feels a little weak. There's another hole in his thigh. He can't remember where it came from. He sticks his finger in and pulls out a few bone fragments--and then a bullet. He realizes he didn't even notice getting shot the second time. He finds a small square piece of metal and jams it into the wound under the skin, hoping this will provide some level of stability.

He walks over to the medicine cabinet and takes three more bottles of Goodknight's pills. He's going to need them. He looks in a mirror and says, "I look like dog shit. I match the TV show now though," and laughs. He stumbles out of the basement and into his car. He doesn't see the taillights of Gody's van pulling away, he doesn't realize that they followed him here.

Some people have a photographic memory, others have a brain that needs a little kickstart to get going. Some people can just recite every word to every song they've ever heard, and others need to hear the first sentence and pick up from there.

Officer Hickox is of the second variety in both classes. He's always had a decent memory, but he needs something to kick it into gear. It's always faces and names he does the worst with. Every time he sees someone he went to school with, he blankly stares at them before saying, "Oh right! You're..." as their name strikes him in his head meat like Babe Ruth hitting a home run.

Before the memory is unlocked, he always feels a sort of haze around his existence. It's like his brain is stuck in some sort of fog and trying to find its way out. He always squints his eyes and tries to turn from his high beams to his low beams.

His eyes were squinting hard when he passed a black Subaru that he thought he recognized. He slowed his patrol car down and stared at it trying to figure out why.

Was this one of his son's friends? No.

Was this a car he pulled over frequently? No.

Did his wife used to drive this car? No.

Goddamnit, he thinks, *what is the deal with this fucking car?*

He turns around in a parking lot and heads back to the lot he passed the car in.

It sits in a parking lot designated for an apartment complex. It's in a section with a sign reading, "Second floor resident parking only."

He pulls up beside the car and looks at it from front to back.

He can't place the damn thing.

He gets out and walks a circle around the car, pausing at the back when he sees something on the taillight.

Looks like dried blood.

Then it hits him.

This car has passed him the past three times there has been violence. It passed him when that couple was killed, it past him at the video store, and the then it passed him during the gunfight. Each time it drives by casually like it just happens to be there. As nondescript as the car looks it makes sense that the driver just happens to be passing through the area.

Not now it doesn't.

No fucking way does it make sense now.

This is someone who's involved.

"Hey," says a voice behind him. "You gonna give this guy a ticket for something? I don't think he's done anything wrong."

"No," says Hickox to the man who has walked up behind him. "Just recognize the car from a few incidents this week. I'm on the murder cases. Do you know whose car this is?"

"I shouldn't tell you, but I'll be damned if I'm letting a serial killer live in the same building as me. I don't know his name, tall dude with blond hair; lives in either 201, 202, or 203. I only know that because he takes a right at the top of the stairs and those are the only apartments up there."

"Thanks, I'll check it out."

He walks to a set of stairs and hears the man yelling, "Wrong set!" He turns around and sees the guy pointing at the set of stairs on the other side of the building.

Couldn't have told me that when I started walking? He thinks.

He can see the guy is too busy filming what's about to happen though. As if he can film through walls.

Hickox walks into the hallway and turns right. He knocks on the first door, 203. He stands there for a bit before giving up and going to 202. When he knocks on 202, he gets a weird feeling. The kind of feeling he gets before shit goes down. He puts his hand on his taser and knocks again. He can feel someone watching him, so he looks around and--sees no one. He decides it must just be paranoia and moves to 201.

A young woman opens the door at 201 saying, "Listen, I told you I'd have rent next fucking week... Oh, sorry, Officer."

"It's ok," Hickox says. "Hey, do you know who lives in the other apartments?"

"Am I supposed to tell you that?"

"Not really. I was just sort of hoping you'd trust I was asking for a good reason."

"Sure, whatever. I don't know names. Dude that lives in 202 is like in comics or something. The couple in 203 have a pay-for-content site. At least, I think they do. I always see them coming in with tons of new shit and I can hear them doing porn moaning through my walls. Sometimes they talk about getting comments and requests and all that shit. I don't, like, watch it or anything. Well, maybe the Easter special where they were dressed as rabbits and laying eggs. Do rabbits lay eggs?"

"Comics, huh?"

"No, it's like... oh. Yeah, guy in 202. He must like them or write them or something. Anyway, I gotta go before my boyfriend shows up. He's into CrossFit and looks pretty good, not trying to brag, just how it is. So, I'm afraid the porn people will try and get him for content. It probably doesn't help that I suggested they should use him... and I would join in. Comic dude was a real dick when I suggested he get my boyfriend the role of Superman."

"Comics..."

The woman pushes past Hickox and heads down the hall.

Hickox looks at 202 and nods his head. A picture is forming and he's going to figure it out.

21

An eye fills the peephole. The all-seeing eye of one Lenny Miller. The eye of a man in pain. The eye that is being held in place only by the swollen and cut skin surrounding it.

Lenny watches as the cop walks away shrugging. That couple from across the hall come out and start talking to him. They cornered Lenny one time and wouldn't stop talking about him doing a comic themed scene with them.

Fucking crazy.

He struggled all through high school to talk to women; now one of them wants to film him having sex with her and her boyfriend for an adults only subscription site.

This comic gig sure got a lot better thanks to *Iron Man*.

Lenny stumbles backward in pain and grabs his arm. The wound is bubbling over; chunks of clotted blood fall to the ground.

"I lost," he says. "I should have won, but I lost."

He falls into the chair at his drawing table. He looks at the panels he drew, the ones where he kicked ass and took names.

He removes the claws from his arm. He digs his fingers into his wound, opening a vessel.

He grunts in anger and frustration. He smears his blood across the page and sticks it to the wound. He grabs a roll of duct tape and uses his old drawing as a makeshift band aid to seal the wound.

When that's done, he looks at the blank page in front of him, a new canvas, a place to start over. He runs his pen across the page creating the image of Robot Ninja. What would he do? If he didn't manage to stop that gang last time, how could he if he ever encountered them again?

He draws the weird girl's boyfriend as Superman fucking the porn couple. One of them is dressed like Poison Ivy, the other is dressed as Cyborg; only who you would think is dressed as who is different. Lenny draws Robot Ninja in the doorway laughing at the woman dressed as Cyborg. Not because she's dressed as a male character, but because he thinks Robot Ninja would have a much bigger robo-tallywhacker than Cyborg. Maybe not... he thinks as he glances at his crotch.

He laughs as he draws Poison Ivy growing a bush that looks like the leader of the gang. He scribbles it out with red pen until he breaks through the page.

"Getcha, getcha, getcha..." he says as he stands up.

He looks at the clock and sees its early morning. He checks his phone and sees a message from Goodknight. Let's fucking go, he thinks.

22

———————

Goodknight stumbles into his basement. He's unable to sleep, thanks to the image of that poor kid he feels partly responsible for killing. He left and went to get a few drinks. He walked and left his car behind, which he regrets now at two thirty in the morning and a mile of drunk walking. Still, he's always been responsible. He couldn't live with himself if he risked someone else's life. Especially children.

He didn't even have to drink and drive to kill this kid though, just give Leonard a fucking suit.

He slips on something and plants his hand on his worktable. It comes back covered in blood.

"What the hell?" he says to himself.

He looks around and finds remnants of Leonard's outfit.

He hits his hand on the work bench and hurries to the medicine cabinet.

"Teufel noch mal," he says as he finds all of the Goodknight special recipe gone. Leonard has lost his mind. He's going to be worse than any of those poor soldiers this was tested on.

He's instantly sober and scared. He shoots Lenny a text. He has to make sure something is done about this. Maybe a face-to-face talk will help. If not, he's going to have to tie him up.

When he opens the door, he feels a hammer hit his stomach and he doubles over.

"What's up, Doc," says Gody standing in his kitchen. "We were going to come by in the morning but then we decided maybe we'd just wait around and meet you when you came out for waffles."

Goodknight looks at the two people in his kitchen completely confused. What the fuck is going on?

"What's…" he starts to ask but he's slapped across the face.

"Don't play fucking stupid with me, Doc," Gody says. "Or should I call you, Robot Ninja?"

Goodknight closes his eyes and silently damns Leonard Miller to Hell.

He brought these people here.

He killed that kid.

The only good that can come from this is feeling like some justice has been served for his part in the child's death.

"See you next fall!" says Gody as she shoves Goodknight backward.

He thinks it was really cheesy how she said that.

That thought covers everything as he falls down the stairs.

He sees the two people step over him.

They start wrecking his basement. They flip the worktable. The man stabs holes in the sofa. The woman picks up the computer monitor and smashes it.

"Hey, Sculley," says Gody. "Check this out."

They're standing in front of the original drawing Leonard made for the costume. The anger radiating from their bodies proves that Leonard has caused this.

"Hey," says Sculley. "Mother Fucker caused us a lot of problems in that. Maybe we should kill us a robot ninja."

"You know," says Gody. "I like your brand of thinking."

Goodknight tries to stand but is kicked in the mouth. Five of his teeth fall to the floor. He scoops them up and tries to put them back in his mouth. He puts one in upside down, the pain is unbearable but he tries to force another one into a socket. When he was a teen he had a wisdom tooth pulled and he got dry socket. Worst pain he can remember feeling, all the way up until now.

Gody grabs him and flips him over. She straddles him and pins his arms down with her knees. Sculley hands her a gun.

"I hate to kill and run," she says.

"I'm… not… Robot Ninja…" Goodknight manages to mumble.

"Sure, well, Goodknight, Goodknight."

Gody puts the barrel of the gun against Goodknight's eye. She pushes it into his eye socket. His eye is smashed back into his brain in complete agony. Gody finally shows mercy and pulls the trigger three times.

Goodknight feels no more guilt for any of his actions, no more regrets, no more nothing.

"Hey, Gody," says Scully. "Check this shit out. Looks like our guy isn't Robot Ninja."

Gody looks around and sees drawings of another guy, a younger guy. He's decked out in the robot fucker gear. He looks a lot like an asshole. He looks more like an asshole than this poor fuck who doesn't have a brain in his head anymore.

"I wonder,' says Gody, "if this stupid prick is as much of an asshole as he looks…"

She picks up a device that looks like a cannon. She puts it on and pulls a trigger. Broken glass shoots out of the barrel and slices up the dead guy's corpse.

"Fuckin' lethal," she says before the duo leaves.

23

Lenny Miller needed a car nap. He needed that special kind of nap where it's irrelevant who's around or what they're doing. All that matters is that you get to sleep. He used to take these kinds of naps in college. Park in a fast-food place's parking lot and zonk out for a while. He was sure there had to be at least seven pictures on the internet somewhere of him snoozing in his car.

The main issue is that when his body decides he needs this nap, he is still driving. He let his foot off the gas and just goes right to sleep like a baby.

Currently a fever dream is playing in his head. He's surrounded by the gang he fought the other day. Some of them are bleeding and crying, others are trying to hold their intestines in their stomach.

He sees the leader, Gody, laughing at him. Laughing because she knows she will always be one step ahead of Lenny.

Not tonight.

Not going to happen.

Lenny charges forward and stabs his talons into her stomach. He rips them upward and slices them back and forth. Her insides pour out looking like chunky applesauce.

She coughs up blood and shredded muscle; it pours all over Lenny's arm.

He stands triumphantly and proud until he hears a voice behind him: "Why didn't you help us?"

He turns to see the couple from a few nights ago, the woman with a massive hole in her face. The kid is there too, only his head looks like a cracked egg.

Lenny feels the weight of failure pressing down on him and he falls to his knees.

He hears the cries fade, replaced by the mocking laughter of the dead gang members.

He sees Sculley perched like a bird pointing and laughing. He's sprouted tiny horns from his head. He's the Devil, he's Lucifer, he is Beelzebub made flesh in a Technicolor dreamscape.

From behind, a creature strangles Lenny with a length of intestine. Another sprays blood in his face from its severed arm. One of the things pulls a long kitchen knife from inside of its thigh and stabs Lenny in the chest.

He tries to fight back and get some leverage against the undead attackers but can find no foothold. He puts his hand on the ground to try and push himself up, but a face materializes in the dirt and bites off three of his fingers.

He finds the strength to free himself of his attackers and stand. When he spins around, all of his attackers have melted together into a pile of fused limbs and gore.

A tentacle shoots out from the mass and stops right in front of his face.

The face of Gody grows from the vile limb and takes a bite out of Lenny's throat.

As he falls in his dream, he wakes up in reality. He's driven off the side of the road into a ditch. He slaps himself in the face a few times and takes some more pills. He searches his back seat for an energy drink. When he finds one, he chugs it in two seconds.

He's got to get to Goodknight.

Lenny drives twenty over the speed limit and swerves in and out of all the lanes. His mind is focused on one thing: getting to Goodknight and getting fixed. His shitty self-repair is falling apart. One of the tubes in his arm popped out and sprayed blood all over the inside of his windshield. He started crying when the windshield wiper wouldn't clean it. *Can't even have windshield wipers that work*, his brain thinks illogically.

Inside his brain he has become Robot Ninja. He feels no more mortal pain. He has no humanity left in his heart or soul. Something has snapped and changed inside of him. Something he needed to happen. Something that was needed for justice. The Robot Ninja has been humiliated by these TV execs, by these other thugs out here killing perfectly happy people. Robot Ninja is now an immortal killing machine. But first, he needs to get better.

He is a robot and the only one who can mend him is the doctor. He can't just go into an ER and get a new battery for his visors. Nothing they can do will make his vision less blurry.

He needs upgrades.

He needs armor.

He needs a health boost.

He knows that the doctor has everything Robot Ninja needs to get back to normal. He'll have the upgrades to help him defend himself better too.

He feels his arm start to seize up like the gears aren't moving anymore. He searches around in the back seat for the oil he needs. He finds a can of WD-40 that he bought to spray on his squeaky door at home and totally forgot.

He jams the nozzle into the open part of his machinery and sprays the substance. It feels like a million hornets have been unleashed inside his nervous system and he screams out in pain.

His arm is working again.

He punches his cars communications device and says, "Tell Goodknight to be prepared, I'm almost there."

"Coming up for the four at four in the morning four way, we've got four back-to-back tracks from—"

Lenny turns off the communicator, which was just a shitty FM radio. Lenny's car doesn't have a high-tech communicator. Lenny's gone nuts.

Message sent and received.

He sticks a finger into the open wound by his eye and flips the switch to enable his heat vision.

The world erupts in pain.

Yeah, his machinery is fucked bad.

He pulls into Doc's driveway.

"Car," he says. "Power down."

He gets out and notices the car didn't listen to his commands. He must really be in trouble if his equipment isn't connecting to his devices.

He walks into Doc's house and stumbles down the stairs. He can feel the gears of his leg grinding against each other in an awkward way. He can feel the belts in his shoulder running off track. His mainframe keeps blurring and turning static sending shockwaves all throughout his body.

He stumbles into the workshop; the place smells like human waste and blood.

He stands on the Doc's hat.

It's covered in blood.

Robot Ninja knows the Doctor would never take off this hat. It's his lucky charm. Only two of these things were made. A custom job for the Doc and his old partner.

Someone is on the floor hanging by their ankles and lightly brushing the concrete floor with the tips of their fingers. Goodnight is hung up like a freshly gutted deer. Blood, brain, and skull matter drip onto the concrete floor. Maybe the Doc is trying out the whole pudding as a living being thing too.

He moves as quickly as he can and tries to help the doctor. He sees half of Doc's head is missing from some sort of explosion; the edges of the wound are burnt. Attached to his chest with a knife is a note that says, *"Robot Ninja fucker meet junkyard."* He laughs a little about the lack of grammatical intelligence. Were they calling him a robot ninja fucker? As in he had sex with robot ninjas? And were they saying to meet someone named junkyard? He knows what the writer meant, and who it was, but his mechanical brain still wanders. Now what should he do with Doc?

Sure, he could rummage up enough equipment to make the Doc a bot like him, but with the Goodnight's mind gone that's the last thing he would want. The Doc would be no more than a mere shadow of his former self. The poor thing would probably spend its entire existence trying to commit suicide in really interesting ways.

He feels his body shutting down from grief. He wants to power down and accept that the evil forces have won.

He can't do that.

He wasn't programmed to do that.

He punches the wall and feels his fingers breaking. The only one that escaped the damage is the only one he needs; the trigger finger. *You lucky bastard,* he thinks as he rubs the finger like it's a lover returning from war.

He stumbles over to the room that Doc has been trying to keep a secret. The room with all of his failed experiments. He sees a picture of Doc and his old partner, both of them wearing matching yellow hats. He sees experiments committed to the human body that belong in a horror film.

A man's head planted onto the body of a bear.

A woman given the arms of a cheetah.

A creature that looks like it came from the depths of Atlantis.

A reanimated corpse.

Lenny shoves all of these things away and searches for more medicine. He needs the medicine. It's the only way his body will survive.

He finds a box filled with bottles of pills. He instantly downs one and pockets five more.

He feels the energy recharging his batteries. That's what he needed.

He finds a package of AA batteries; luckily his visor takes that size. He jams two into the hole by his eye socket. *No wonder I can't see*, he thinks, *there isn't even a battery in the socket.*

He walks confidently now. This repair may only be a band aid, but it did its job.

He finds two devices on Doc's work desk. One looks like an attachment for his visor and the other looks like a metal plate attached to a spring. He reads Doc's scribbled notes about each one. He picks up the plate and attaches it to his arm. He moves his trigger finger into position.

He attaches the small device to his visor and pulls it over his eye. He plugs the wire into the side of his machinery and instantly a crosshair fills his vision. He focuses on the center and a red laser shoots from the device.

These assholes are going to pay for what they did to Goodknight.

Hickox's finger hovers over his siren switch. He almost turns them on more than once but then he realizes, *This guy doesn't know I'm behind him.*

He's been following the Subaru since it pulled out in front of him. It's been driving in the opposite lane more than it's been in the right lane.

Hickox reaches for the CB. His hand stops just short of it. He wants to do this one on his own. He has to do this on his own. He doesn't know who this guy is, but he at least needs driving lessons.

The car pulls into a driveway. A man in a costume gets out and says something. He looked confused and studied his body.

He looks awful.

He looks like he fell into a pit of spikes and got up like nothing happened. If he drank a glass of milk, he would become a milk fountain.

That's a weird thought, he thinks. *What the hell would you even use a milk fountain for?*

He looks at his radio again.

Should he call for back up?

What if this guy is meeting the gang?

He was fighting the gang, though.

He sits in his car thinking about what to do when he hears a door slam. The costumes weirdo is standing in front of the house. He has two new weapons and a bad attitude it looks like.

He walks to his car and slams his face down, covering his head with his hands.

Hickox turns pale when the guy throws his head back and lets out the most primal scream he's ever heard.

This wasn't the scream of a man.

This was something more.

This man was a creature of some sort.

A ghoul.

The car drives away, and Hickox hesitates to follow. Maybe someone inside can tell him what's going on? Maybe he can kill some time before attempting to fuck with whatever that was.

He gets out of his car and makes his way up to the doorway. He has his hand on his pistol the whole way. He opens the door and stares down into a darkened basement.

He takes the steps slowly, the smell of blood and burnt plastic filling his nostrils.

When he reaches the bottom, he finds the place has been turned upside down.

There's a man hanging from his feet with a letter pinned to his chest.

The place looks like a factory used to build Terminator or something; gore and machinery everywhere.

"Shit," Hickox says before turning on his radio. "I need back up at the junkyard ASAP."

26

Robot Ninja knows his gears are out of whack. He can feel the belts misfiring. Every time he takes in Carbon Dioxide from the air, he can feel something in his chest stopping the flow. He was built to inhale what man exhales; in this way he is like a tree. A tree made up of pain and violence. In some ways, maybe he'd prefer being a tree. It feels as though there is a rock in his lungs, the breath pauses for a second before exploding past whatever barrier is there. He thinks about trying to do surgery to fix it, but only the Doc has ever messed with his internal machinery.

He knows his voice commands aren't working anymore either. With that in mind he doesn't bother trying them on his car. He just pulls up and shuts it off.

When he gets out, he takes a picture of himself with his cellular communicative square. He sends a few pictures of himself to the people who are documenting him on TV. He attaches the message, "This is a tough battle today, I wanted you to see the real face of Robot Ninja, not the cleaned up one for the cameras. I detailed this mission on paper as well. You will find them in my charging station."

He throws the square into a puddle before it can receive a reply that reads, *"Lenny, this some kinda fuckin joke? Where R U? Is this cosplay or some shit? By the way, we hired a new artist for the next run. UR GETTING FUKN WEIRD MY MAN."*

He can smell the vile scum in this junkyard. He can smell atrocity after atrocity. After he's finished them off, he really needs to try and find some replacement parts.

He sees three men standing around a fire laughing about how much of a chump Robot Ninja is. They think they're going to take him out before he gets to their leader.

They're wrong.

They're about to find out how wrong.

He places his finger on the trigger of the device he's now calling the face smasher. He strolls over to the three men as confident as a dog getting a treat for taking its daily shit.

He doesn't even give the men time to realize he's there. He puts the face smasher against the back of one man's head and pulls the trigger.

The impact is instant. The man's head didn't even have a chance to move forward with the plate. It just smashed through the back of his skull and into his brain. His eyeballs pop out of his head and a red substance that looks like mashed potatoes pours out of the sockets. The eyeballs bounce off one of the other guy's chest.

The man falls forward and Robot Ninja can see the other two staring at him in shock.

"Holy shit!" one of them says. "Mother fucker snuck up on us."

Robot Ninja feels something wooden hit the side of his face. A man is holding a baseball bat. He points the face smasher at him and realizes it hasn't retracted. It just sort of dangles there as the man hits him over and over again with the wooden bat.

He hastily undoes it and tries to discard it, but he's hit by another bat in his arm. The face smasher is sent sailing into the fire. He looks at the guy with vengeance in his eyes. Only got to use the damn thing once and it's already fuckered.

He turns to the man who just hit him and swipes out with his claws. The guy jumps back and hits him in the chest with the bat. In a way, this is a benefit. Whatever was stopping his breathing has come lose. He feels something travel through his lungs and fall out somewhere along the way. A hole is better than a blockage any day.

Robot Ninja falls backward and lands beside the fire. He sees a glass bottle glowing from the heat. He grabs it with one hand while putting the now retracted face smasher on the other. He leaps off the ground like a wild animal and pins the man with the bat to the ground. He places the scorching glass bottle against the man's nose. The smell of his flesh melting is only rivaled by the smell of Robot Ninja's flesh melting inside the face smasher.

Before he can pull the trigger, he's hit in the back of the head by another bottle. He spins around fast, knocking the guy to the ground. He points the smasher and pulls the trigger. It smashes the guy's testicles into the ground. The man screams out and rolls in agony.

By this time, the other dickhead is up and throwing punches. Robot Ninja turns and says, "I see through you,' before shooting a laser into his enemy's chest. A hole slowly grows through his body. It looks like germ sized piranhas eating away at his body. Blood cooks and evaporates before it can even drop to the ground.

The injured criminal crawls across the ground on his belly. Robot Ninja can't allow him to escape and get help. He shoots the laser into the ground behind the man and slowly raises it between his legs, then through his torso and head. The man now lays cut in two down the middle, his wounds seared.

Robot Ninja notices that the laser has cut into his ear. Something must have gone wrong and some of it shot behind his mask, his ear hangs on cut in half.

He sees the plate of the face smasher still glowing red from the heat.

He presses the metal against his ear hoping to seal the two

halves back together. Instead, he melts the two halves to the side of his head.

He opens a pill bottle and downs all of the medicine.

27

____

Sculley couldn't believe what he had just watched. That fucking guy took out three guys at once. What was with the eye? Was he that guy from The X-Men? He didn't want his face to go all melty like that other sad sap. He wiped the sweat from his face. A bead dropped into his eye and felt like a bee sting. He flexed his arms and shook out any hesitation he had.

This mother fucker has got to die, he thinks. He watches at a distance as the costumed clown places the side of his head on the red-hot metal. He doesn't even scream as it burns him.

You know, maybe I don't want to fuck with this guy, he thinks.

He remembers last month when he tried to rob that guy. Gody made him go down and threaten him with a bottle. Sculley punched the guy in his face and--nothing. He broke the bottle over the guy's head to no reaction at all. He picked up a brick and cracked the guy on the head; he just stared at him and grunted.

"You know what," Sculley had said. "I don't think I want to fight you anymore."

The other guy wasn't of the same mindset. He beat Sculley all the way up, down, left, right, right, left, down, up, hold the L and R buttons and press Start, into a cheat code. Apparently, it was God mode because the guy was invulnerable.

When he told Gody about the incident she kicked the shit out of him. He had never seen someone so deceptively violent. She threw him down and kicked him in every spot he had left open. His balls hurt for weeks, and he still thinks he sees a little blood in his piss.

One fuck up, two ass kickings.

Math ain't mathing.

So, the choice is, fuck with crazy guy, or take his chances with Gody.

He shakes his head, grips the handle of his knife, and marches toward the fucking Halloween decoration.

He watches the Robot Ninja stumble and fall backward. He dumps a whole bottle of pills in his mouth, and he's back up.

Sculley hesitates again, surely there's a better way.

He slaps himself in the face a few times and says, "Come on Sculley, goddamnit. He's more fucked up than a football bat!"

He strolls toward the guy with the confident swagger of a businessman who knows he can't lose in this deal. His father used to tell him to dress for the job he wanted, but how do you dress to kill a guy dressed as a fucking robotic ninja. *What a stupid thing to have to worry about,* he thinks. *Cops? Sure. SWAT? Sure. A guy pretending to be a fucking robot that also knows karate or something? This guy is a chump!*

He tosses the knife back and forth in his hands. All he has to do is get close. Guy can't aim that laser up close. That fucking Nut-Smasher 3000 is a whole different story, though. He thinks about attacking from the other side, stabbing the guy before he can react.

"Well, well, well," he says. "Looks like I get to kill a robot ninja!"

He pulls back the knife to stab the fuck. He realizes this was supposed to be a surprise attack and, just like the time he told Gody he loved her, his mouth is going to cause him blood loss.

He feels three knives jam into his stomach. The hand makes a swiping motion and all of his insides come pouring out. It feels like he's just taken the biggest shit of his life.

He tries to scoop them back in but it's no use.

He motions for the man he was previously going to kill to help, but he walks away.

His last thought is that he should have taken his chances with Gody.

28

That armadillo TikTok song is a real fucker. It burrows into your head for weeks at a time. Then, when you need it most, you can't remember how it even goes. It's stuck on your head, but at the same time can't be stuck in your head because you don't remember the way it goes.

The Fortnite song is similar, only that one is always accessible in the mind. That one doesn't require a search; it's just there ready to be used. It's an ear worm that takes up residence.

Kind of bad ass how memory works like that. The human mind can just conjure up anything it's experienced. Sure, it's a shell of the actual experience. It's still there though. What happens when you learn something new, though? Is the mind like a bucket and when you put something new in, something else pours out? Is that where the armadillo song went? What if you lose some really important shit?

The thumb of Officer Milton was losing its fingerprint from scrolling. He kept swiping, knowing that damn song had to pop up eventually. He's not concerned with the knowledge he has pouring out of his brain. Most of that is about Porn Hub links anyway. Losing the memory of one Sara Jay video in trade for that armadillo song makes sense right now. He needs the armadillo song. He doesn't need Sara Jay.

Couldn't he just search for it? Hell yes. But he didn't want to. He wanted to find it organically.

Ohhh wee... no.

Go little rockstar... no.

My life, my rules... no.

Goddamn this was harder than he thought. This is worse than the time he couldn't find that video of the teenager crying because his brother was moving out.

"I love you, I'm sorry, please stay here with me."

Fucking armadillos!

The monotony of life.

"Armadillo—"

FINALLY!

The video was cut off by his phone ringing.

"FUCK!" he yelled. "Yeah, what?"

"Turn on your radio dipshit!"

Click.

Goddamn Bianca could be such a bitch! It's not his fault she works like ninety hours a week to take care of that bratty little shit-kicker kid. He even tried to date her once and she turned his ass down. *Must not want too much help, huh, mom?*

He turns on his radio and hears officer Hickox requesting backup at the junk yard. The junkyard he's parked at.

Weird.

Almost like it was meant to be.

He gets out of the car and places his hand on his firearm. He didn't listen to the whole report but assumes it has to be serious.

He walks into the junkyard and looks around.

Nothing but junked up cars and appliances.

He sees something moving inside a dilapidated dryer.

He aims his gun.

A rat jumps out and runs away.

He points his gun at the rat as it scurries.

He doesn't really plan to shoot but he wants to fuck with it.

Would the rat even know? Probably not.

When he passes the open path in front of him, headlights come on.

A car spins out as the gas is laid down heavily. He can see it's a black van. He points his gun at the vehicle and shoots.

He misses.

He tries to move but his pant leg is hooked on a bumper. Some abandoned car making sure he's a blood sacrifice.

He tries to undo his pants, but he doesn't have enough time. He looks up with just enough time for a song to pop into his head.

Armadillos keep digging holes, in my back yard…

That's the song! He thinks as his body is crushed between a three-ton van, and a wall of junk.

He tries to breathe through his crushed lungs but all he can muster is spitting up blood.

A woman climbs out of the van and points a comically over-sized gun at him. "Let's see what it does to fucking pigs," she says.

A broken bottle shoots from the barrel sending chunks of broken glass all through his body. He can't feel the shard pierce his eye, he can't feel his tongue getting cut in half, he doesn't feel his own finger thud against his forehead after being separated from his hand. The only good thing about this event is that he doesn't hear the laughter coming from Gody.

Humans are wasteful bags of meat. They're made up of mostly water and calcium. It's a wonder they don't burst like balloons from just walking around. Without some sort of upgrade, the human body is about as worthless as a tennis shoe being used as a sledgehammer. The human brain may think it can do certain things, but the body will disagree. Humans are stupid.

Take, for example, this one that tried to stop a moving vehicle with his body. He's just a pile of red mush now. No upgrade in the world can fix that.

Robot Ninja shakes his head from his hiding spot. He can't process through his motherboard why this man thought he could stop a van that was driving at least sixty. Robot Ninja probably couldn't even stop that thing. He wouldn't explode like a bag of gelatin, though.

He tries to switch his visor to heat vision, or "Predator Sight" as he calls it. "Want some candy?" he says to himself as he leans over a pile of junk. He slaps the side of his helmet, and it does nothing.

Stupid thing is fucked.

He realizes it doesn't really matter; he can see just fine anyway.

He jumps down in front of the van just in time to see Gody step out.

"Well, lookee here," says Gody. "Got the fucking Halloween bandit all to myself. Tell me your name before I fuck you up?"

"I am Robot Ninja," he says. He does a spin kick that clips Gody's chin sending her stumbling back. "And I kick ass."

"Goddamn. Look at you. You're more fucked up than a Christmas lasagna served at Easter. We're talking one foot in the grave and the other in Crisco."

Gody moves fast, faster than she should be able to. She punches Robot Ninja in the back of the head and sends him falling forward. He rolls over and kicks her in the gut. She stumbles back slightly but keeps moving forward. She's like a tiger who senses her prey is weak.

Robot Ninja stands up and punches her in the jaw. She looks to the side and spits blood before punching Robot Ninja on the tip of the nose. She moves in fast as she kicks him in the side of his thigh sending him to one knee.

Robot Ninja baits Gody in, just like when you're playing Mortal Kombat 2, and then he hits her with an uppercut. The annoying strategy of a shitty little brother.

"Fuck off, robo-bitch!" she says as she moves forward and stomps on his right foot.

Robot Ninja feels bones shatter and he lets out a small scream. A scream he realizes is unnecessary as he can't even feel the pain.

He stands to his full height and slices his blades back and forth at Gody. She dodges every swipe and moves in to strike like she's playing *Punch-Out*.

Robot Ninja starts to stumble as he swipes. His body is starting to feel some of the pain from his injuries.

He feels the tissue in his right leg rip apart. He stumbles forward and feels his leg. There is a mix of torn flesh, muscle, bone, and glass. He turns to face Gody, she is aiming the canon at his face.

This can't be, he thinks. *I'm a machine, not a man.*

He looks at her and fires a laser at her head. She dodges to the right and a red light behind her explodes. His vision slowly notices another light behind her. A spinning blue one. He looks to shoot again; this time he needs his legs under him. He tries to stand but his destroyed leg can't hold his weight. He collapses to the ground screaming.

Gody sees him hesitate and moves fast. She punches him rapidly in the face. His visor flies off into the junkyard. His nose begins to feel like a water balloon.

She aims the cannon at his face and prepares to pull the trigger. A smirk crosses her face because she knows she has won.

Blood and bits of her skull make it to Robot Ninja's face before she can take the shot.

He hears gunshots and blood flies from her head and chest. Someone is shooting.

He scrambles to his feet and shuffles behind the wall of junk. He uses the shooter's distracted demeanor and makes his way back to his car.

As he fires it up, he sees the same police officer that was at his apartment in the headlights.

He pushes the gas and realizes he's starting to feel more like a man by the minute.

Robot Ninja is malfunctioning.

30

The gears are slowing down.

The main frame has been fried.

The wires are all burnt up.

Robot Ninja has no more little pills of salvation.

He needs to be fixed and there's no one on Earth who is capable of doing it. Doctor Goodknight was his creator, his Doctor Frankenstein. No one else is as capable of fixing his fried machinery.

He drives his car into the parking lot of his home. How is it that a machine has lived among these humans and never been noticed?

His vision is blurring with every single step he takes toward the building. He stumbles and tries to catch himself with the arm that's missing its hand.

He slaps the arm hoping to get the electronics back in order. Instead, sparks shoot out of the end. What does it mean when electronics have red sparks? Can't be good.

He stumbles up the stairs and into the hallway leading to his home. If he can get there, he can plug in for a bit and feel a little better. Maybe then he can mend himself just enough to get by.

He sees a trail of oil following him; just like the sparks it's a deep red.

A door opens and a woman steps out. "Hey," she says. "Are you rethinking- HOLY SHIT CALL THE COPS! CALL THE COPS!"

She slams her door hard enough that Robot Ninja falls into his own door. His weight breaks the lock and handle. If he wasn't on death's door already, he'd be a little concerned about how unsafe this is.

He falls to the floor of his apartment. He crawls over to the charging unit. When he plugs it in the charging port in the front of his stomach, he feels nothing.

He looks around the apartment and sees drawings of himself all over the walls. *I must be pretty self-absorbed*, he thinks.

Oh no.

It all hits him like a shotgun blast in the nuts.

He feels his brain start to fuzz at the realization. All of a sudden, every wound on his body starts to come into focus. He falls back in agony and screams out. The agony of flesh and mind melding together, creating the reality of what has happened. There was never a Robot Ninja.

He's done.

He let people die.

He's going to die.

Robot Ninja is going to die.

He crawls across the floor. His hand plants onto the TV remote. The *Robot Ninja* show pops on the TV in some sort of cruel joke. He sees his life's work presented as a cheesy, overly animated bargain bin version of a Marvel movie. On the screen Robot Ninja is making bad one liners and dodging lasers.

Lenny reaches into a drawer beside his recliner and pulls out a handgun.

He points it at the screen and shoots. The TV blows up in sparks and fire.

He puts the gun in his own mouth.

I created it, I can end it. He thinks. *Just as it should be.*

31

———

If this fucking guy doesn't stop getting away from me in that goddamn Subaru, I'm going to blow my brains out! Hickox thinks as he drives down Main Street toward the apartment complex.

He arrived at the junkyard and found bodies everywhere. He didn't know what to do or say. He found a fellow officer turned to stew between a van and a pile of mangled metal.

He heard the yelling. He jogged around a corner and found the woman from every scene pinning someone down. She looked like she was about to deliver a killing blow to the poor person's head.

He didn't want to miss his chance to end all of this, so he aimed and pulled the trigger.

When the gun went off, dust blew into his eyes causing him to blink. He wiped it away and fired again.

The body was down.

He assumed both people must have been killed until he got over to them and found just one.

He buzzed in for other officers and said he was in pursuit of a vehicle. He jumped in his car and took off.

He knew where he was going.

When he got to the apartment complex, a call came over his

radio. Someone called 911 and reported that a neighbor looked to have been assaulted. They also said he was wearing some sort of Halloween costume.

Got the fucker, Hickox thinks.

He runs up the stairs. He passes the online porn girl and her partner. Her partner is more concerned about the content than the violence. He's rubbing her body all over and Hickox swears a nipple popped out.

He sees the doorway open and slowly steps in. He aims his gun around the corner letting whoever is in there know, he is armed and a little pissed off.

"Hey!" he yells. "I know you're in here. I'm armed and a little pissed off. Just come out. Let's talk this over."

He finds Lenny on the ground.

The man is no more.

Hickox sits on the ground and leans against a wall. He inhales and exhales deeply.

If only he had just been a little earlier.

He held his son a little tighter that night.

CHAPTER 32

A warehouse door explodes inward. Metal rains down on the group of lowlife scumbags who kidnapped Robot Ninja. A man standing six foot five inches with two hundred and fifty pounds of pure muscle walks in. He's wearing a completely mechanical suit; it resembles an exoskeleton.

He grabs a man buy his collar and throws him out of the new entrance. The man can be seen flying into the clouds in badly rendered CGI.

The machine man moves into the warehouse and eliminates all of Robot Ninja's captors. He throws them through the roof, drops them into portals, and turns them into puddles of water using his hand cannon.

When the crew is gone, the machine man squats by Robot Ninja. He picks up his head and holds him close like a mother holding a newborn.

"Please," says the machine. "I need you. I don't know what to do. I always need you with me."

Robot Ninja taps on his chest over his heart. A microchip slides out. He pushes the microchip into the new machines chest and says, "Now you will... Mecha-Samurai..."

With that, the scene fades on Mecha-Samurai holding Robot

Ninja and weeping. Text appears on the screen that reads: *"Follow Mecha-Samurai's journey every Thursday at 8 PM! Right here—"*

The screen shuts off and two voices can be heard talking.

"I fucking knew that guy's hands were insured for a reason!" says a man's voice. "Even if he is an asshole!"

"His comic is SO much better," says a woman's voice. "Way better than anything that Lenny Milner made."

"Miller."

"We only have Coors."

"No, no. Miller. Lenny Miller!"

"Oh, that's right. Who needs him anyway."

"Have you seen that bird site? New dickhead owner has to limit the number of posts people can view because so many people are talking about this!"

"Yeah… a lot of them are mad though."

"Who gives a shit! They're going to watch the show anyway!"

"Too true, too true."

"And that actor! I knew hiring a professional wrestler was a better idea than an actual actor!"

"His voice is so SCARY!"

"Er, well, actually... that's not his voice. We got this other guy to do the voice... guy sounded like a chipmunk."

"I want a hoola hoop!"

"They're at least happy we included the in-memoriam part for Lenny. A lot of these goofs think the guy was a hero."

"A psychopath more like."

"Batman, Shatman, who cares! He's still making us money in death!"

"Even more money!"

"Hey! You know what you should do? You should make a workout video based on horror movies!"

CHAPTER 33

In a cramped, dark, smelly, moldy, shitty basement, a hand drags a pencil across a blank canvas. The hand creates a new hero. The Mecha-Samurai! The hand is attached to an arm with a hefty insurance policy. The arm is attached to a man. A man who is tasked with filling Lenny Miller's shoes. He doesn't even know what brand the guy wore!

He never thought his little pitch at the big comic office would work. But here he is. Making up his own character to replace that overrated asshole, Robot Ninja.

My creation, my sweet baby. He thinks. *You have canons, knives, swords, throwing stars. Not to mention a fat ass and a bad attitude.*

The hand cramps having not fully recovered from the injury. The hole in the middle making him feel as though he has suffered some form of stigmata.

The man looks back at a darkened closet and sees the busted mask Lenny Miller wore when he went on his vigilante killing spree. He sighs and stands up. He walks over to the mask and pushes a button on the side.

The whole closet lights up in red. A mechanized exoskeleton powers up and stands. The mask glows green and the visor is blood red. The damaged half has been sawed off and replaced with a single glass screen that covers the user's eye.

The man looks at his creation and says, "Now, let's see if a Mecha-Samurai can do better than a Robot Ninja."

The man tilts his head back and pours a bottle of pills down his throat.

As he laughs maniacally, the pained voice of a reanimated Doctor Goodknight can be heard from the next room crying over a lost hat.

AFTER CREDITS SCENE

The comic shop was packed. The final issue of *Robot Ninja* by Lenny Miller arrived last night and had already sold out.

All except one that is.

The special golden foil addition sits under the glass counter. The light reflects off it as the man at the counter licks his lips thinking about the profit he's about to make on it. If only the fucker would sell!

A woman moves through the store looking over back issues of *Robot Ninja*. She picks up a few TPBs and grazes through collectibles.

The clerk recognizes her from somewhere, but he can't quite place it. Maybe high school or some shit.

She grabs a replica Robot Ninja hand claw and tries it on. She flexes her fingers a little and shakes her head. She grabs a replica of the Lasso of Truth and smiles.

She comes to the counter and sets it all down. She points to the special edition and says, "I want to get that too."

The clerk opens his eyes quickly. *Big spender we got here, huh?* He thinks. He rings up all of the merchandise and bags the comics. The woman takes the lasso and attaches it to her belt loop.

"Last issue of this," he says grabbing the special edition. "This is the one Lenny made before... well... you know..." The clerk points his hand at the side of his head. He makes a gun shape and pretends to kill himself.

"He did it in the mouth,' the woman says. "Out the back of his skull. Haven't you read Hickox's book?"

"No, ma'am, I haven't."

"What's that?" she says pointing behind the clerk.

"That's the Trident of Atlantis."

The woman looks at the end of the lasso like she's thinking. Finally, she says, "I'll take that too."

The clerk grabs it and rings it up. "It's made out of steel," he says. "Hella pricey, but supposedly as close to the real thing that Aqua-"

"That's fine," she cuts him off.

"Ok... that'll be three thousand seventy-six bucks."

She hands him a card.

"Hey," he says. "You got a loyalty program here? You could get some big points on this purchase."

"Yeah," she says. "My little brother made me get one so he could use it." She looks sad. A small regrettable smile crosses her face like she's remembering a lost loved one.

She sighs and speaks...

"The name is Christina Moulton."

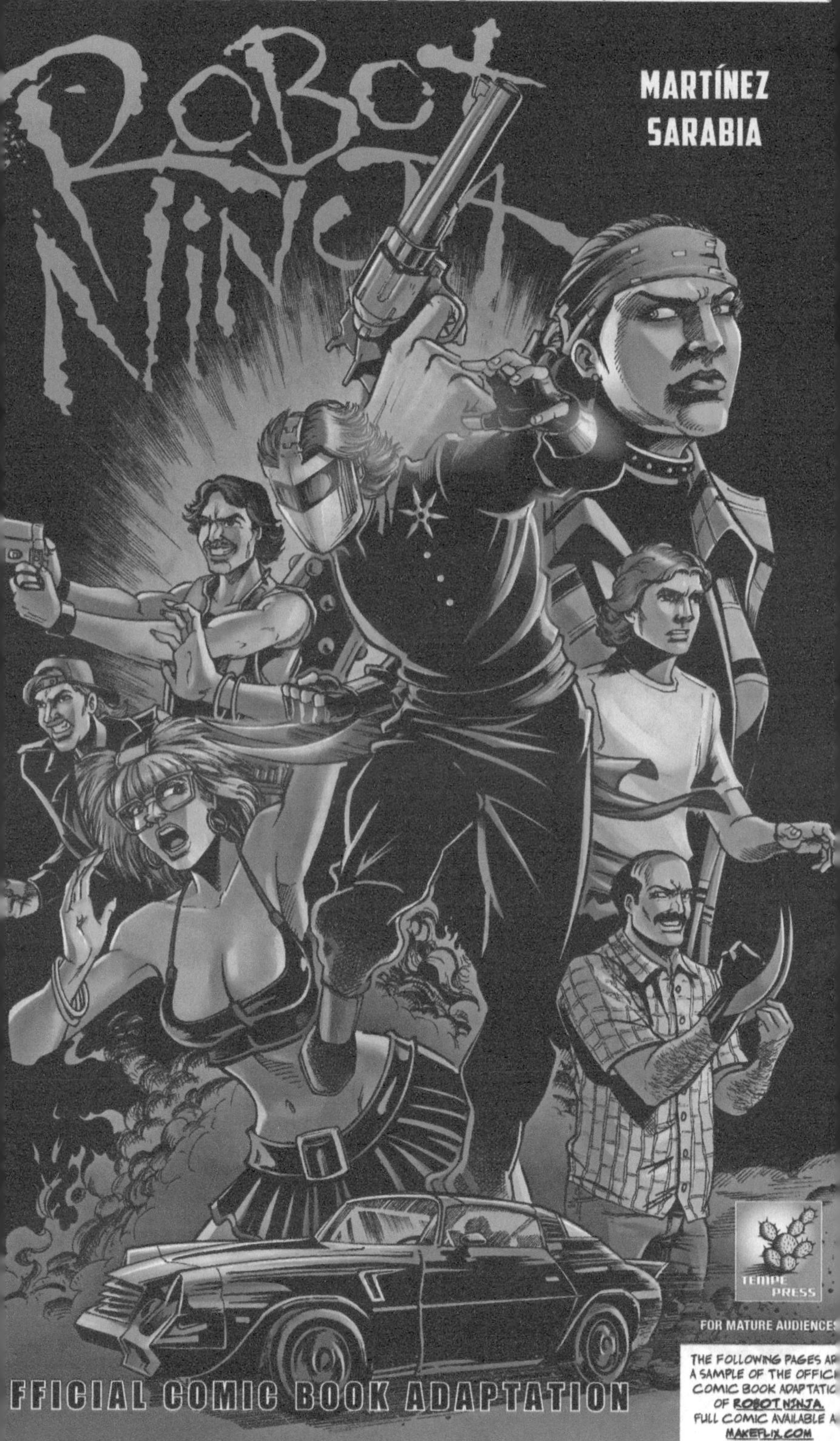

ROBOT NINJA
MARTÍNEZ
SARABIA
TEMPE PRESS
FOR MATURE AUDIENCES
FFICIAL COMIC BOOK ADAPTATION
THE FOLLOWING PAGES AR
A SAMPLE OF THE OFFIC
COMIC BOOK ADAPTATIO
OF ROBOT NINJA
FULL COMIC AVAILABLE A
MAKEFLIX.COM

SCREENPLAY:
ABRAHAM MARTÍNEZ

BASED ON THE FILM WRITTEN BY:
J.R. BOOKWALTER

ROBOT NINJA CREATED BY:
DAVID LANGE

SPECIAL THANKS:
SVETLANA
BENJAMIN
SOPHIA

WAYNE ALAN
HAROLD

VECTEEZY.COM

PENCILS:
ALEX SARABI

INKER:
JESÚS SALAS

LETTERING & LAY
LANCE RAND

COLOR COVER:
CARLO CHAB

INSIDE COVER PINUP:
ARTURO LOUGA

ROBOT NINJA Official Comic Book Adaptation Vol. 1, No. 1, Winter, 2018. Published by Tempe
a subsidiary of Tempe Entertainment. OFFICE OF PUBLICATION: P.O. Box 212, Uniontown, OH
0212 USA. All contents copyright © 2018 Tempe Entertainment. All rights reserved. All characters fe
in this issue and the distinctive names and likenesses thereof, and all related indicia are property of
Entertainment. No similarity between any of the names, characters, persons, and/or institutions
magazine with those of any living or dead person or institution is intended, and any such similarity whi
exist is purely coincidental. Printed in China. Based on the motion picture "ROBOT NINJA" directed
Bookwalter, available from Tempe Digital. Visit our online store at tempevideo.tictail.com for more cool

LATE ONE NIGHT IN SUBURBAN RIDGWAY, OHIO...
CRACK!
UGH!
SNIKT!
WHO ARE YOU?!
I AM THE ROBOT NINJA...
AND REMEMBER, KIDS: DRUGS ARE NOT COOL!

THE ROBOT NINJA SHOW
AND TO THINK LENNY WAS OPPOSED TO DOING IT CAMPY LIKE THE OLD "BATMAN" TV SHOW!
HA HA HA HA HA!
OH BOY, THIS IS THE BEST DEAL I'VE EVER MADE...THE RATINGS ARE SOARING!
"IF ONLY I COULD SEE WHO'S BEHIND THE MASK..."
HE HATES THE SHOW!
HA-HA, I WONDER WHAT HE THINKS ABOUT THIS EPISODE!
"TUNE IN NEXT WEEK... SAME NINJA-TIME, SAME NINJA-STATION!"
EXIT
LENNY! HEY... UM... H-HOW YO DOIN'... I... UH...
THIS SHOW IS HILARIOUS!
I HEAR YA, BUD... I HEAR YA!

CUT THE SHIT, RIP.
WHAT'S THE DEAL WITH THE TV SHOW?!
I'M HERE WITH THE PRODUCTION GUYS.
C'MON, TELL THESE GUYS WHAT YOU THINK ABOUT ALL THIS!
RIP, I'M THE COMIC BOOK ARTIST. YOU ARE MY AGENT.
DO YOUR JOB!
OK McHEISTER, LISTEN... WE THINK YOU SHOULD...
NO, YOU LISTEN! AMSCO COMIX GAVE US THE RIGHTS FOR THIS SHOW. I KNOW HE'S THE COOLEST CHARACTER SINCE TMNT...
BUT WE'RE MAKING A REAL ROBOT NINJA --
NOT SOME COMIC BOOK VIGILANTE!
YOU DON'T GIVE A SHIT ABOUT ROBOT NINJA!
DO WHATEVER YOU WANT ON TV... I'LL SHOW YOU WHAT ROBOT NINJA IS REALLY ABOUT!

STOP IT!
DON'T DO IT!
DON'T DO IT, HERO MAN!
LEAVE HER ALONE, YOU SON OF A BITCH!
BLAM!
UGH!
RUN, SUSAN... RUN!

BLAM
BLAM
BLAM
WHOOSH
EEOO-EEOO-EEOO-EEOO
THE COPS ARE COMING!
LET'S SPLIT!
NO!
NO, DAMN IT...

HERE'S THE NEW LIZARD BOY PAGES, MR. KANE.
HAVE YOU SEEN THESE ROBOT NINJA PAGES?
TWO HORRIBLE MURDERS! GUNS! THIS DOESN'T LOOK LIKE THE TV SHOW...
PLEASE CALL LEONARD.
HI LENNY... YES...
I THOUGHT WE AGREED TO DO THE NEW BOOK LIKE THE TV SHOW...
YES, I KNOW THE COMIC BOOK IS YOURS...
WHY DON'T WE RELEASE THIS NEW STORY AS A GRAPHIC NOVEL?
LENNY! AS SOON AS YOUR CONTRACT ENDS WE'LL HAVE A SERIOUS TALK --
CLICK!
"ROBOT NINJA..."

HELP ME, DOC.
YOU'RE AN INVENTOR!
I THINK THE SUIT CAN FREAK 'EM OUT LONG ENOUGH FOR THE POLICE TO ARRIVE!
PLEASE DOC, FOR ME. I CAN PAY FOR IT.
GOD FORGIVE ME...
OK, I'LL MAKE IT.
"IT'LL TAKE A FEW DAYS AND I'LL NEED SUPPLIES FROM THE HARDWARE STORE..."
BZZZT
"..IT WON'T BE CHEAP..."
FZZK!
"...AND IT WON'T BE COMPLETELY LEGAL..."
"BUT IN THE END, YOU'RE GONNA LIKE IT."
CBM

The following pages include various poster art used in the promotion of Robot Ninja as well as images from the film. Used by permission.

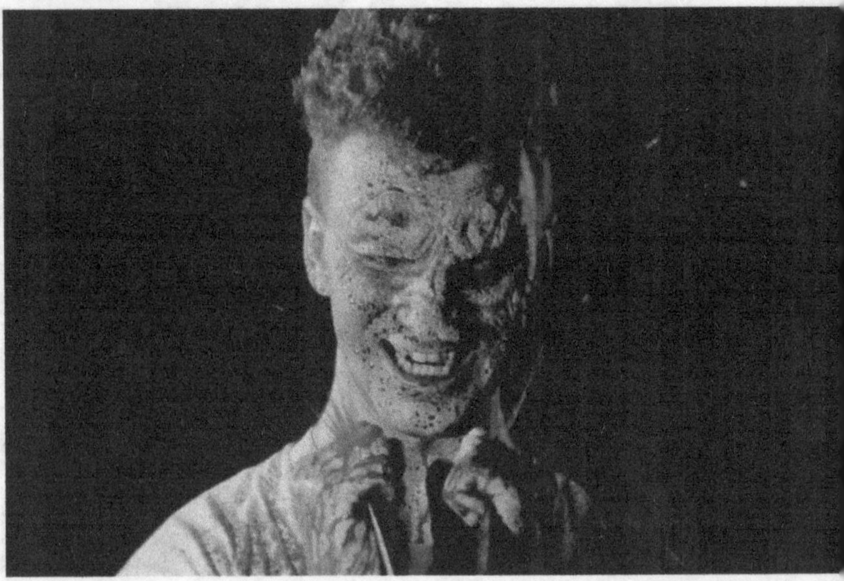

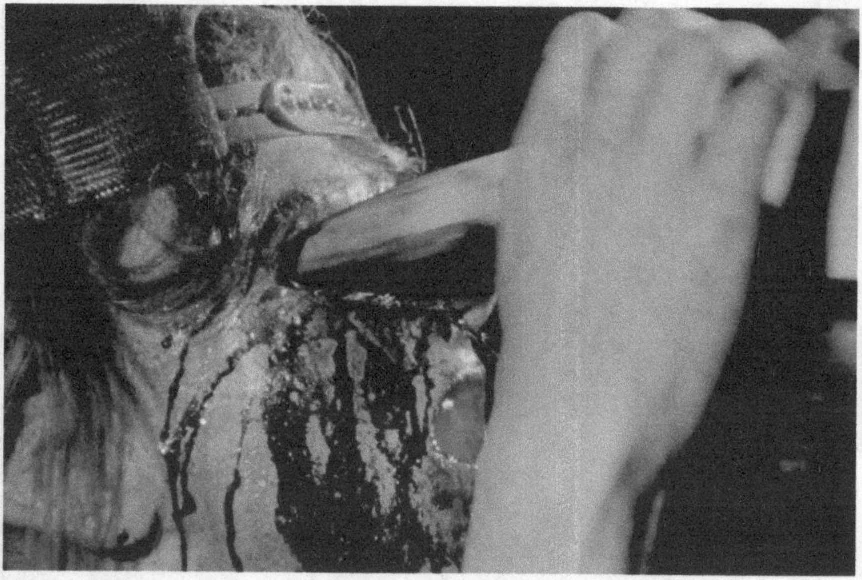

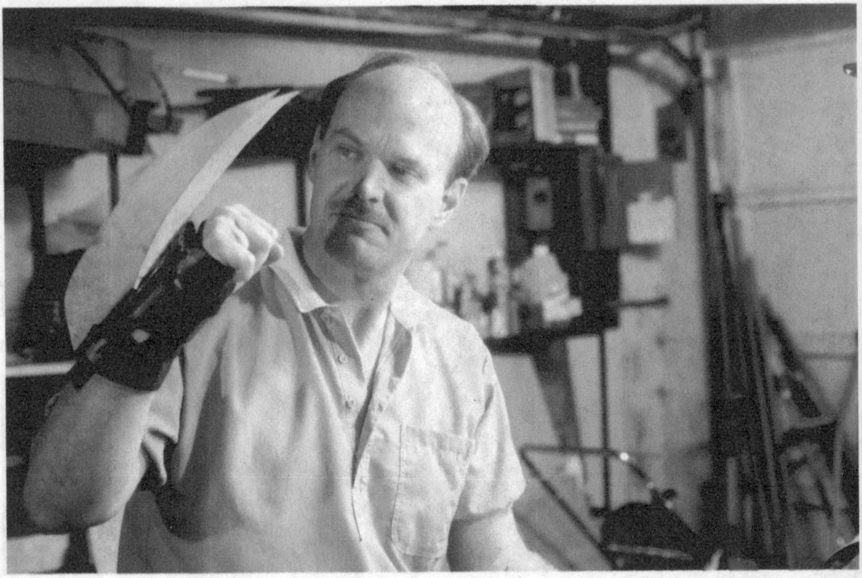

COMING TO
AMERICA
ON VIDEOCASSETTE

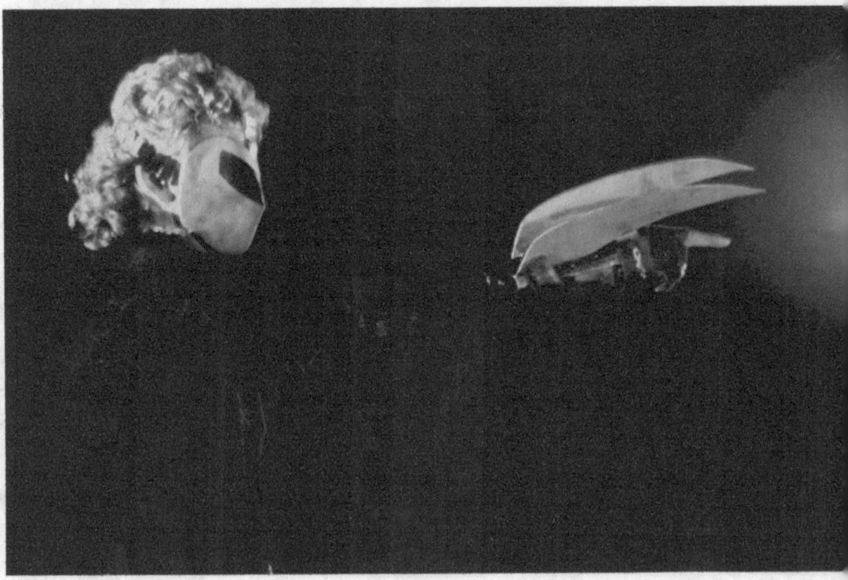

HAT'S LIVING
EVISION
WAKES UP,
DEAD

ABOUT THE AUTHOR

Damien Casey writes horror comedy. He was made when some guy threw a bunch of b-movie and wrestling vhs tapes in a bonfire. K THX.